Dear Leaves,
I Miss You All

To
VAL & RON,

Dear Leaves,
I Miss You All

Sara Heinonen

S. E. Hei——

Mansfield Press

Library and Archives Canada Cataloguing in Publication

Heinonen, Sara, author
    Dear leaves, I miss you all / Sarah Heinonen.

Short stories.
ISBN 978-1-77126-020-6 (pbk.)

    I. Title.

PS8615.E36D43 2013   C813'.6   C2013-905610-6

Editors: Stuart Ross and Denis De Klerck
Author photo: Tom Ridout
Typesetting: Stuart Ross
Cover Design: Denis De Klerck

The publication of *Dear Leaves, I Miss You All* has been generously
supported by the Canada Council for the Arts and the Ontario Arts Council.

Mansfield Press Inc.
25 Mansfield Avenue, Toronto, Ontario, Canada M6J 2A9
Publisher: Denis De Klerck
www.mansfieldpress.net

For Eric
李展光

Contents

THE EDGE OF
THE WORLD

TABIT'S DAD WAS ABOUT TO JUMP. We spotted him as we passed the high school we had just graduated from. Other men in sweats were jumping too. One by one, they sprang from the brick wall of the front entrance to the hard dirt below, a drop of six feet. I recognized what they were doing from a documentary I'd seen about parkour. Tabit's dad landed, then grabbed the wall and crab-walked back up. He hopped around while he waited his turn, his bright white teeth broadcasting unadulterated joy.

"Not again," Tabit said, and bit at her fingernail. She was dressed in another monochromatic outfit. This time it was blue. "That's the second day of work he's missed this week."

Maybe her dad's behaviour had provoked her recent foray into drugs. There was also George, her boyfriend, with his brooding intensity and evasiveness and his flute ballads. They were always breaking up. I worried she might fall apart.

We continued along the sidewalk until we heard someone running to catch up. "Hey! Hey, girls!"

Tabit's dad's workout pants hung off his hips. His face glistened. "Did you see my jump?" His bulging eyes swam laps from me to Tabit. "It'll be on YouTube later."

"Maybe it'll go viral," Tabit said.

He nodded and grinned, as if she was serious. Tabit's dad was a lawyer representing people in reality television. This sounded mildly impressive until you spoke three words with the guy. He'd blather on about nothing we could make sense of, as if that was the best he could do with the maelstrom in his brain. He often listened in on Tabit and me discussing world events—floods, storms, earthquakes, bankrupt nations, leaking nuclear plants—and though he didn't contribute anything coherent, at least he looked concerned that the rest of the world writhed in agony while the citizens of our privileged country grew increasingly apathetic. Recently he'd asked about the book I was reading on agnotology—the study of how our culture makes us ignorant—but I gave up explaining when his crazily tapping feet indicated that he wanted to go jump off something.

"You gonna come watch us?" he asked.

"Sorry," I said, and held up a DVD. "We have something planned."

What the hell were we doing, Tabitha and me? Traipsing through the humid days between the end of high school and the kickoff to our official lives, the adult part. I'd been accepted to a university in another province to study sociology though I had reservations about leaving my mom—she'd lost her job and was spending time in a nest with an owl, thanks to the wonder of webcams. Tabit was planning to study political science at a university out of town and I was trying to help her keep her shit together a few more weeks, long enough to get there, where I knew she would flourish.

I was working the summer in an ice cream parlour, a sticky, lobotomizing place that brought out unsavoury qualities in the mostly middle-aged customers—indecision, greed for toppings, eager, grasping hands. Tabit got a few shifts each week in a veterinary clinic. She said the best part was petting the fur of sleeping animals when no one was looking. George busked in the financial district. He'd been making more money than any of us, possibly more than our underemployed parents. George said business people flowed out the mirrored towers at noon to gather around him. He alternately played his flute and sang about the importance of thinking independently and staying hopeful. The business people chomped on hot dogs and listened, hanging off his every lyric. Some even swayed. Burdened by food and drink, they clapped with their forearms, like seals. Before disappearing back into the towers they dropped ketchup-speckled bills into his open case. Tens and twenties. The odd fifty. But George had noticed that lately his earnings had begun to dwindle, just like the number of business people. Every day, a few more of them would wander off down the street instead of going back to work. "It's such a betrayal," he'd told me. "I'm sharing my innermost thoughts through music, and each day another dork stops paying attention."

When Tabit and I weren't working we circuited between our houses and the library, where we borrowed books and films to keep our minds sharp. Today I was carrying *Gorillas Speak!*, a documentary about teaching sign language to a young gorilla named Betty.

Tabit and I sat in her basement sipping Scotch and eating crackers and brie and exchanging shocked glances. Betty's captor, a large-eyed scientist with a stoner's moronic smile, babbled to the camera about the gorilla's extensive sign language vocabulary. Holed up in a drab trailer, Betty was alternately praised for her human-like efforts and scolded for her gorilla-like inclinations. The deal-breaking scene, the one that made us spit crumbs of outrage onto the carpet, was when the scientist gave Betty lipstick, only to admonish her for smearing it across her forehead. I kept willing Betty to hurl the scientist against the kitchenette and make a break for the distant trees. But, of course, the trailer was locked.

Tabit turned the DVD off. "I was *already* feeling hollow today," she said. "That didn't help."

"I can't believe that shit was Criterion," I said. I rattled the ice in my glass, considering the wisdom of another drink.

Tabit got up. From a vase of plastic flowers she pulled out a little bag of pills. She was small but her neck was thick and her face the kind of pretty that drew stares. Today she looked tired. She'd been up journalling the night before. Through stream-of-consciousness writing she was trying to get at her core emotions. This was fine but I wished she'd ditch the drugs—though she had been saying insightful things lately. For example, she said the reason our parents could no longer function was they recognized the futility of applying themselves to a diminished world. They had lost heart and given up.

Tabit plucked a blue pill from the bag and swallowed it dry.

"You're at blue now?" I should have guessed from her outfit.

"I've *earned* blue, Shauna," she said.

The illicit pills came in a series of colours based on karate belts—white, yellow, orange, green, blue, brown and black—each colour progressively more potent and demanding. With intense focus and heaps of positive energy, reaching the black level promised self-realization, though temporary. To her credit,

Tabit was not a mess, not yet at least, and I hoped that university would put an end to the pills.

She selected something on the iPod dock and baroque string music swelled through the room, an *allegro* piece so uptight it was cool. She danced, which for Tabit meant shaking her fists with her feet planted on the carpet. Her exquisite face conveyed both bewilderment and hope, like she was searching for a book in the library.

After a brief crescendo the music stopped.

"Fuck," she said, "I need to get outside."

George leaned against the porch railing, trilling away on his flute. He wasn't quite pulling off the quasi-bohemian look he had going: faded jeans and a loose cotton shirt, his frizzy brown hair almost to his shoulders. His chunky build and rosy complexion suggested a recent home-cooked meal even though nobody's family bothered anymore. Nightly we faced pasty food microwaved in plastic containers.

"New tune," he whispered, his blue eyes sparkling.

Tabit bounded past him and down the steps as though freed from a leash. "Not here, not here!" she said. "Follow me on the path to enlightenment!"

"She's at blue now," I explained.

Hot sunlight sliced through the trees. We moved through the soupy beams and back into the shade as we sped to catch up with Tabit.

Surrounded by quiet streets and houses, the park was just a couple of trees stranded on a big rectangle of weeds that looked more or less like grass. We sat down near where the play equipment used to be before it fell apart. The neighbourhood's evening routine was underway. Food delivery cars pulled up and kids walked stir-crazy pets and teens throbbed in clusters along the sidewalks while the white-hot sky turned the pink of raw meat and the humid air clasped the back of my neck. George played his flute until shouting erupted at the centre of the park, where two paths crossed. A skinny man in a suit stood swearing at nobody. Then he slammed his briefcase into a garbage can and stormed off.

"Nice suit," George said.

"It's the economy," said Tabit, voice trembling. George reached over and stroked her hair. "Everyone's either ditching or dejected. They want to be productive but they've lost not only their will but their means. Anyway, why be productive? How is it of value, existentially, to contribute to an economy that's morally bankrupt? I mean, fuck."

"What if it's a bomb?" I suggested, because I kept looking for signs of unrest, of apathy sprouting into frustration, then violence. The garbage can remained inert. In the distance the angry guy got smaller and smaller until he looked like a twig.

"I've never worn a suit," George said. He lived with his mother and sisters, so it wasn't like there was one around to borrow.

"Imagine this," I said. "You're wearing a suit while all the business people listen to you on their lunch break. You're singing about breaking free of the rigid corporate mentality but now you're in a suit just like them. Maybe if they see that they can *be* like you and still *look* like themselves, maybe then they'll hang in there."

George nodded. "I like what you're saying."

"He'll lose his otherness," Tabit said, her voice still wavering. "I don't want to see you in a suit, George."

But the idea crackled in my mind. Seeing George transformed. Seeing him rise above everyone and do something important we couldn't even fathom. He had money now and therefore choices, and not all of us were so fortunate. Maybe I was selling myself short. That was possible. Maybe I was in love with George. That was possible too.

It was dusk. I got up and offered my hand to Tabit, who was wilting as the pills wore off. She let me pull her to standing while George blinked up at us.

"What's next?" he asked.

"Something grown-up," I said.

I led them through my front door, but Tabit went only as far as the living room, where my mom had left damp laundry draped everywhere. Mom would be in bed with her laptop watching the owl's nest in a northern forest while socializing online with her friends, even though they all lived nearby. She had made noises about scouring for a job but my guess was she did nothing. She spent a lot of time staring at the back of the owl's head, waiting for it to swivel and offer her its unblinking eyes. Tabit plopped onto the couch, remote already in her hand. A noisy shoe commercial invaded the room.

George followed me upstairs to the spare bedroom where my mother had put all Dad's clothing and CDs and sports equipment. After a decade's absence, it was unlikely he'd be showing up to use it. Either he's a tragic figure who died far away, alone and unable to contact us, or he's a cold-hearted genius who saw that things were on the skids and cut his losses. George stopped outside the room while I opened the closet and slipped a dark grey suit off its hanger.

"Try it on," I said.

"Whose is it?" He didn't know much about me or my family.

"If it fits, it's yours."

George put the jacket on. It fit although he couldn't button it across his wide chest. I held out the pants. He unzipped his jeans, looking at me with a mixture of pride and nerves. I just kept my eyes on his while he dropped his jeans and put the pants on. They were too long so I knelt in front of him and folded up the hems. While I was down there he cupped his hand lightly to my hair. I stayed still a few seconds, thinking about what he was thinking. His hand like a bookmark for a moment we might return to in the future. But when I stood up we both acted as if nothing had happened. He took stuff from his jeans and put them in the jacket pocket.

"Now what?" he asked.

"It's your first time in a suit," I said. "Make it count."

I had no idea what I wanted him to do except to be serious and also open to infinite possibilities.

On our way out we passed Tabit. She was asleep and we paused to look down at her.

"Someone should paint that face," George said. "I mean, for a painting."

On the television a group of wrinkled blond women took turns interrupting one another. They sat on mauve chairs and their gesturing hands flashed jewelry and vibrant fingernails. I couldn't pick up on the topic but one of them said, "Our power as humans, girls, is in our ability to decide."

"I can't believe it," I said to George. "She's quoting Buckminster Fuller."

Then the woman added, "But how can we do that when no one is pointing us in the right direction?"

George snorted as he picked up his flute and led the way out to the porch.

George and I sat on the front steps under the darkness of the trees. I like watching the night sky, and when I can't see it I get restless. Recently I'd watched a documentary on Buckminster

Fuller. He said some fascinating things about the universe. The one that blew my mind was that some stars we see are actually dead. It takes many lifetimes for light to travel the vast distances to reach our eyes and during that time some of them kick the bucket. They shine along with all the still-alive stars and, just looking at them, we can't tell them apart.

"I like the way this feels," George said, pulling me from my thoughts.

"You mean nighttime in summer?"

He tugged the sleeve of the jacket. "The *suit*, Shauna."

George blew a few throaty notes on his flute. Though I find his music interesting—his songs meander, no discernible melody or chorus—I wasn't in the mood to be left essentially alone while he communed with his art. He played awhile, then lowered the flute and sang: *"Do you remember your life at work? Life with work? Oh, life, it is work. Do you remember the money earned? That you dropped at my feet? Dollar bills at my feet."* And here his voice rose high and sharper—his signature sound— *"Oh, sweet money for my tunes!"*

I was ruminating on the change in George's lyrics—less philosophical than I recalled—when the vibration of a truck lumbering up the street pulsated through the steps and upstaged his song. The truck groaned to a stop in front of my house. Strapped to the side were ladders and, on top, a flashing light that made the leaves overhead jump from orange to darkness and back again. Three workers emerged. They wore hard hats and fluorescent yellow vests. One of the guys gripped a flashlight and a clipboard that he read out from. The two others started lifting up sheets of plywood we hadn't even noticed were spread around on the road. They slid sheet after sheet off to the side.

"I wonder what they're up to," George said, standing.

"It's just nice to see adults working," I said.

One of them took a ladder from the truck and slid it into what we now realized was a big hole in the road. He stepped down and disappeared below the surface.

"Down, down, down," George said, jingling coins in his pockets. "That sucker is going *down*."

I figured he'd pick up his flute and segue into song. Instead he slowly exhaled. The street was silent for a summer evening. There was no one on the sidewalk, no one driving by. I pictured everybody in the neighbourhood glued to their televisions and watching the blond women on the plush chairs. Maybe they had been saying something important and we were missing it.

The guy handling the pylons set the last one on the asphalt and stepped onto the ladder. We watched his hard hat descend out of view.

"They must be fixing it up," George said.

"How do you fix a hole by going *into* it?" I asked.

The one with the clipboard clomped around on the pavement. He stopped and shone the flashlight down the hole, then started writing. He climbed back up into the driver's seat and stayed put. Several minutes later there was still no sign of the others.

George straightened the suit jacket, flicked something off the lapel and walked over to the road. I followed. Near the curb was a gaping pit bigger than the area of two cars. The ladder stuck up out of it. We couldn't see the bottom.

"A sinkhole," George declared.

"But sinkholes occur because of an underground disturbance," I said. "Usually after a storm or some kind of utilities construction. Nothing has happened here."

"Maybe our focus should be on solutions," he snapped, "and not speculation."

I looked at him. "What the hell's eating *you?*"

Just then a helmet broke through the darkness. We moved back as one of the guys climbed up and out, then another. Ignoring us, they pulled up the ladder and hooked it onto the side of the truck, but they didn't put the plywood back over the hole. The engine started up.

"Excuse me!" George called, pointing. His grey, suit-jacketed back was as rigid and imposing as a slab of granite. "You're just leaving this here?"

"Do we look like Road Repair?" one of them said. "We look like we have *asphalt* ready to go?"

"Clearly this is a serious hazard," George said.

"Who the hell are *you?*" The man's sneer was like a slight not so much against George as against the suit.

"I'll be contacting someone about this," George continued. "I have friends downtown who'll be interested to know about holes in the road big enough to swallow *an entire goddamn community!*"

Shaking their heads, the men hopped up into the truck and drove off.

George strode right over to the edge of the hole and looked down.

"*Someone* has to get to the bottom of this!" he yelled in. The hole did nothing to his voice. I was disappointed for him. Like any of us, George just wanted to feel significant.

He came back onto the grass.

"George!" Tabit padded across the lawn toward us. "George in a suit!" She caressed his back.

"He's going to wear it when he busks," I said.

Tabit clutched his shoulder and started laughing. She laughed so hard she snorted but she still didn't let go of him.

"What's so funny?" I asked. George wasn't laughing. He removed Tabit's hand like it was debris.

"That isn't how he makes his money," Tabit said.

"Hey, Tabit," George said. "What the fuck?"

"What's going on?" I asked.

He rubbed his forehead, then shrugged. "I've stopped going downtown. I don't busk anymore. I deal."

Deal? I reeled from the sucker punch of his complicity in Tabit's Little Problem. Meanwhile she had noticed the hole and stepped toward it. Luckily, George saw too and we lunged in unison, just managing to grab her thin arms.

"It's okay!" she shouted, trying to wriggle free. "I'm solid. I'm not transcending anymore."

George's admission and the strain of holding her were pissing me off. My arms ached. But although the three of us, huddling there, would never be this close again, George's gaze skimmed the top of our heads as if he was imagining a future that wasn't great, maybe, but big and challenging, a future he was going to take on.

Tabit broke free and got right up to the edge. George stayed beside me, hands in his pockets, watching her.

"Stop her, George!"

"Tabit," he said, and as he yanked his hands free a plastic bag fell out. Dozens of black pills spilled onto the grass and asphalt.

Tabit crouched at the hole and stared down in. Both her proximity to the edge and the revolting black pills, like the blind eyes of dolls, brought a ribbon of bile up my throat. Despising both George and Tabit, I twisted away and hunched over the grass, though all I produced were a few pathetic dry heaves.

From the front door my mom's carefree voice sailed out: "Hey, you guys! Want some dinner?"

I almost believed she was offering to cook. Then I saw the phone in her hand.

"We're in the middle of something," George shouted at her.

She came right out in white socks that would get filthy. "The middle of what?"

George grimaced up at the dark trees. "Please. Just go inside."

"*You* look very grown up!" Mom said to him. George straightened up. He did look older in the suit. I could picture him at thirty, forty, fifty years old all at the same time. I wasn't sure I liked what I saw.

"We're not children any longer," he said. "Far from it. We've got a firm grasp of the current state of affairs out here."

She had nothing to say to that.

When she'd gone in we turned back toward the hole, but Tabit wasn't there. Then we spotted her, halfway up the street walking home. George stopped staring after her and started pacing.

"I can't fucking believe you!" I said. "Are you that much of a creep all of a sudden?" He sure looked like one, squeezed into that suit jacket, pant cuffs unravelled and dragging on the pavement. "How could you screw Tabit up like this when she's worked so hard to get into university? It's her one chance to get away! She's lucky her dad's still working and can actually help pay. I mean, she has this real chance to improve the world a little! Seriously, George, what the fuck is wrong with you?"

"Maybe, Shauna," he said, "you should be asking what the fuck's wrong with Tabit." He gazed at me. In the gloom of the streetlamp his eyes were gaping pits. "They're only sugar," he continued. "I have real shit but I wouldn't give her that and she knows it. It's all just make-believe."

"Wow, George. Like I'm going to believe that."

"Don't then. But it's true." He looked at the ground. "Those were the last of the black ones. She'll be disappointed. She was pretty hyped to earn them."

Then it made sense. This was a game, a coda to end their adolescence. I began warming to the idea of harmless sugar pills. There was, however, Tabit's brilliant rant about political reform and democracy in the Middle East when she was at orange level. How was she coming up with that stuff?

"Then she's amazing," I finally said. "Some of the things she's been talking about have really amazed me."

"Yes, and she'll be even more amazing in the future," he said. And before I could say anything else, maybe about how I, too, might be amazing, George held up two fingers, either the sign for peace or "V" for victory. At any rate, he left. He walked away with the suit but left his flute on the porch.

Now it was just me and the hole. I yanked at the plywood and dragged it across, then sat on the curb. I wanted to be certain no one fell in. I sat a long time. I'm not sure why I felt responsible. Just like I did about Tabit, who was my best friend. She'd go to school, she'd be okay. She'd been okay all along, really, even though she'd been keeping things from me. But I'd been keeping something from her too. I wasn't leaving in September. I hadn't gotten the scholarship, and going into major debt in another province while Mom imploded back home just didn't seem like a good plan.

The neighbourhood houses gradually went dark while the streetlights glowed and hummed. The air smelled like leaves and humidity and overwrought flowers and people sleeping obliviously in their homes. When a raccoon walked by and hissed at me, I moved up to the porch where I could still keep an eye on the plywood. A while later Mom came out. She'd made me a sandwich.

"Is this okay?" she asked. It was only yellow lettuce on stale bread but the effort was encouraging.

I was hungry but also exhausted. I ate half and had to close my eyes for a second.

I must have dozed off because when I looked around Mom was gone. The plywood appeared to be in the same position but I couldn't be sure from way up on the porch. Part of the hole may have been exposed. What I hoped was that Mom was safe in bed with the nest. Now that it was dark the owl would be preparing to head out for a night of hunting. Before leaving, she would swivel her head and stare into the webcam with those eyes like black moons on yellow skies. And then the owl would turn away to face the world because she has things to do out in it. She flies up through the darkness, wings pumping, cool night air streaming over her feathers. She leaves the dark edge of the forest, flying first over the snaking line of the river, then coasting over a field of silent silver grass, her wings stretched wide to the horizon. She decides to do something new. There's still time before the business of hunting. She tips one wing up and pivots, until she is coasting upside down, belly to the endless sky above.

ULTRA

———

RON SLOUCHES IN THE SWIVEL CHAIR and presses the Play button with a socked toe. He has convinced Cassandra from Deli to come up and watch something unusual on the security monitor from the morning's power outage. The monitor shows Aisle 5 in infrared mode. Shelves of ketchup, cooking oils, Saran Wrap made eerie by the lack of light and shoppers. Several seconds pass before a middle-aged woman with short brown hair appears pushing a loaded cart.

"So this was just after it happened?" Cassandra looks at Ron's neatly combed hair, detects a minty scent in the air.

"Just before they got the generator running. They'd already evacuated."

"Then what's she doing still inside?"

"Hang on, just watch."

The woman abandons her cart and charges down the aisle and out of view. Ron hits a button to show Aisle 6, likewise deserted except for the sprinting woman. She stops at the laundry detergents, removes several enormous boxes from the bottom shelf and crawls into the cavity. Her arms appear and reposition two boxes to fill the gap. And she's gone.

"Okay, that's weird."

"You haven't seen the best part." Ron reaches for Cassandra's waist, but she twists away.

"You have thirty seconds to show me. I'm not even on break. I said I was going to the washroom."

"Patience, Cassandra. Keep watching."

I lay in bed listening to the incessant and unusual squeaking of the cardinal that woke me. It seemed like a sign. I turned to look at Benny, half-asleep, with one arm shielding his eyes from a stripe of sunlight. "Since when have cardinals started sounding like two pieces of Styrofoam rubbed together?"

"How can you talk that way about a bird? Jesus, Barb, it's nature."

I got up and pulled on a T-shirt and shorts. What could a change in song signify? An environmental imbalance? Something about to happen? I felt compelled to make an unscheduled inventory of my emergency provisions in the basement room where I store cans of tuna, beans, potatoes, soup, bottled water. Several shelves had been emptied. I shot back upstairs and Benny confessed that he and our son, Carson, had hauled off a few dozen cans to a community food drive. I would discuss the provisions issue with Carson later. On Saturday mornings, he was usually teleconferencing for the two organizations he ran from his bedroom (world peace and the preservation of some bird species—not cardinals, thankfully). He was planning to spend that day making his birthday piñata (a combat tank to be whacked down from the basement ceiling, then burned on the driveway; the day before, when he'd tried to explain the underlying political statement, I had left the room, overwhelmed). He'd promised not to turn the party into something huge like the earthquake-relief benefit in our living room that necessitated hiring an engineer (our home's structural load: maximum two hundred and fifty people, seated or standing still). Carson was turning eleven.

The time will come when my family will gush gratitude for my foresight. They will survive because of it. All I ask is that they respect my efforts to prepare for the emergency that will surely one day test our wits and resources. The newspaper on our doormat suggested that day had arrived—*Electricity Grid Overburdened, No Foreseeable End to Marathon Heat Wave, World Oil Supply Past Peak, Province on Terrorism Alert.* After a quick, nutritious breakfast I was off to Ultra-Store, a five-minute drive away.

It took another five minutes to cross the parking lot past shoppers pushing huge rattling carts under a sky that was a whitish-grey composite of heat and smog, a sky with no suggestion of how the day should be spent, a whatever kind of sky, like the environment giving the finger right back at us. The leaves of the puny trees were browning. The expansive sidewalk was a large griddle capable of cooking people before they could get inside to the food. The automatic doors, opening and closing, repeatedly sighed a one-note mantra, or was it a warning? Maybe a hymn. With an extensive restocking list, I was looking at minimum forty minutes in Ultra-Store, a grocery store gone mad. A loathsome place. An airport hangar with Spiderman underwear, six flavours of pomegranate juice, marinated beef kebabs, fitted bed sheets, flax seed oil, Tensor knee braces, citronella candles, Egyptian tomatoes, frozen nan bread, ant traps, novelty socks, forty types of deodorant, and starfruit from Indonesia. With brilliant lighting reaching into every corner. No place to seek shade. I could only brace myself and shop.

My cell rang. Or played, rather: one of Carson's compositions that he programmed into it.

"Hello?"

"Can you pick up a few things from our regular shopping list?" Benny calling.

"Well, the cart will be full of restocking items, but I'll try to squeeze something in." He would recognize my pissed-off tone and its subtext: how dare you compromise our safety by decimating the provisions.

He said, "Bagged milk, one per cent," and hung up.

"Good morning, shoppers! Wondering what to serve for dinner? Pick up a box of breaded chicken bits from the freezer aisle. They're every bit as good as fresh!" The voice cut off and the store soundtrack resumed with a Madonna song Benny had sung badly at a karaoke bar on our honeymoon.

Approaching the bottled waters, I was distracted by a man staring at boxes of licorice. He looked vaguely familiar, maybe Joel Wallingford, who used to hang out with Benny and me at Scarborough College. At first I wasn't sure if it was him—the slackened chin and pouches under the eyes, the faded Roots T-shirt and cargo shorts. Joel used to gel his bleached hair into explosive shapes, wore wacky shirts and tartan pants. The guy turned and stared, caught, like me, looking ordinary in middle age.

"Barb?"

"Joel."

"Wow, you live around here? I've never seen you."

"I tend to keep a low profile."

"Ha, ha!" His outburst earned the stares of several weary

shoppers. "So, how're you doing? Man, it's got to be—what—fifteen years? What are you up to these days?"

"Just some geotechnical consulting. Dirt and aggregates, nothing special." I dismissed my life, flicked it away like lint from my shirt. As Benny has pointed out, my home-based business has withered in reverse proportion to my burgeoning hobby: collecting information on humanity's progress toward self-annihilation.

"And how's Benny-boy?"

The image of a charming young Benny popped into my mind, surprising me. Benny Morton, the moderate one, the one who eased Joel and me and others back from the edges of things. Like intriguing drug offers or arguments with sharp-tongued drunks in clubs. Benny, who led us back to our homes to sleep or, in my case, to bed. In our current marital state as distracted housemates, it was too easy to forget.

"You knew we finally got married? We have a son."

"Fantastic. Well, as you can see I'm still standing, still breathing." He sucked in a great gulp of air and, on the exhale, added: "Married too. Third time." He shrugged and looked around, as if to locate family members or a shopping cart. "So this is fantastic running into you. We should get together. I'd love to see the Ben-meister. Has he changed? What about his amazing hair?"

"Benny is still Benny, though with diminished hair." Recently, I'd trimmed his crazy halo of brown curls in an attempt to make it proportional to his bald spot.

"Benny's the best. The best." Joel shook his head in awe.

I nodded, wanting a wrap-up—I still felt like strangling Benny, after all.

Joel's gaze drifted to my cart. "Man, Barb, you doing some serious cooking or what?"

29

"Just stocking up."

"Yeah? I should do that."

"Not enough people realize the importance of provisions."

"*Provisions?*" he burbled.

"Well, yes. You never know when something might happen." I couldn't stop myself.

"You mean, like fifty people show up for dinner?"

"No, something catastrophic. Like a collapse of the food distribution system, which is vulnerable, to say the least."

Joel indulged in a rippling laugh that rose in pitch and volume. Passing shoppers smiled at us as if they'd rather stand around with a goof like Joel—who once convinced me to skip a mid-term soils test to hang out with the guitarist from the Meat Puppets—than get their shopping done and get the hell out of there.

Tears formed in his eyes. "Barb, you're something. I'd better get going, but email me, *okay?* Joel100@hotmail."

It would be okay when I got away from him. Carson's music played from my purse like a miracle.

"I'd better take this call."

"Don't forget: Joel100@hotmail."

"Absolutely."

He bounced away on the balls of his feet.

It was Benny again. "Jesus, Barb. Here's what I need for dinner: two pounds of stewing beef, onions, green pepper—"

"Whoa. You're making a stew when it's forty-five with the humidex." Surely if I laid the facts in front of him, he would see his stupidity.

"I'll turn on the air. I'm in the mood for hearty." Possibly a comment on my recent foray into beans and tofu: eating low on the food chain.

"Unbelievable." I rolled my eyes at a passing woman, desperate for a witness to my husband's inanity. "There's no way

I'll supply you with the ingredients for an irresponsible meal. You know damn well why not." I hung up.

Benny and I had an understanding about the air conditioner. If he turned it on, I'd leave the house in protest against burning coal to relieve us from excessive heat caused, in part, by burning coal. Carson was with me on this and could be counted on to don his "PULL THE PLUG ON WASTE" T-shirt, though he did remain in his cooled room. I'd been meaning to talk to him about this.

I made a sharp aisle turn and almost rammed my cart into Joel and the loaf of bread he carried. I managed a smile and kept going.

"Code 99 to the shipping dock."

I moved through the store, following my list and watching customers reach for things they probably hadn't come to buy. I watched their pace slow to the Valium tempo of the soundtrack. If they weren't careful, they might forget to leave. I pushed my cart, hearing the staccato beeps of the cash-out scanners layered over an irritating Tina Turner song I'd spent twenty years trying to forget.

I was reaching for a can of chickpeas when I felt a breeze on my neck, heard the squeal of a cart at my heel. Benny with a red face and bulging eyes. He must have raced over. A Benny this pissed off was an unusual sight. I hesitated to break eye contact but had to see what was in his cart: three trays of stewing beef and a bag of brownies that wouldn't make it through the car ride home with him this stressed. He started grabbing cans of tomatoes like a delirious game-show contestant.

"I've got the air on and it's going to be the perfect temperature when I get back to make a humongous pot of stew. It's going to be simmering for *hours.*" An elderly couple glanced up from their shopping list, frowning.

"Did you not feel the temperature out there? *We* are simmering, Benny. The world is on the brink of crisis and we need to be thinking of survival, not comfort. But go ahead. Cook a stew on the hottest day of the goddamn freaking millennium. I'm speechless."

"Code 400 to the shipping dock."

I looked around, but no one was acknowledging the apparent escalation of codes.

"No, you're neurotic is what it seems to me. And you're making Carson neurotic too. I don't even know what the hell either of you are talking about half the time."

"I'm shopping to protect our family. Call that neurotic, if you want. And who's looking after Carson, by the way?"

"June is checking in on him after she cuts her grass. But you, Barb, you are really getting screwy."

"Screw you, Benny!" I turned, heart sinking into my gut, and met the horrified stare of a woman who was covering the ears of her toddler. Had we been yelling?

Benny stormed off with his cart, the drama hugely diminished by how long it took him to pass the rice, pasta and boxes of Kraft Dinner. I headed the other way, not caring where to. I ended up in front of a fridge loaded with the Pepperettes sausage snacks Benny adores. His family's cardiac history being what it is, I only buy them for special treats.

"Hey, Barb. Benny's here too." Joel was beside me holding a kielbasa. "I bumped into him on his way in."

"We're fighting."

Joel put the kielbasa back like it was something he would have to earn first. He fixed me with a steady gaze. "Fighting is part of marriage. And it's okay as long as you keep the love flowing too. Otherwise"—he pretended to pull his hair out—"it's hell."

"My marriage isn't the problem, Joel. The problem is that nobody seems to see the big picture."

"You're right. It's *all* about perspective." For a moment he stared at the display of plastic deck chairs beside the pasta fridge. "Email me, Barb. We should talk." He walked off with his bread.

I could hear little voices singing the alphabet out of synch and turned. Two girls in purple jackets were crouched beside the deli counter. They stopped at "P" and started over. Behind the counter, a young woman yawned and weighed a tub of potato salad with a blank expression. *Cassandra,* her name tag read, the italicized letters suggesting cheerful vitality. She slapped a sticker on the lid and looked at the clock as she passed the tub to the customer. Imagining the tedium of her job, I considered my own relative freedom. Benny had done well with his hockey store, well enough for me to pursue my research. That got me thinking about Benny's good qualities: his unsinkable optimism, his tolerance of things he didn't agree with. Maybe I was being too hard on him. I picked up some Pepperettes and hid them in my cart.

I found Benny in the cookie aisle. "Remember your heart. You have to limit the saturates."

"Barb. Sweetie." He put the double chocolate chip cookies back and reached for my hand. His eyes were damp. "*That's* what I need. I need you to show me you still care."

"I do, though. I always do."

"Good morning, shoppers! Be sure to visit our dairy section and sample our new Stringy Cheese flavours. Don't forget to pick up the Ultra-Pak and save."

"No, you're focused on practical things. Like that spreadsheet on survival strategies. You don't pay attention to me."

"What kind of attention do you expect when you take off with half the provisions?"

"It was a food drive! I didn't take, I *gave.*" He shook his head as if to clear the subject away. "Barb, we have to keep the love flowing."

"So you bumped into Joel Wallingford too. What's with him?"

"He's a good guy. He cares about us, even after so many years."

"Let me know when he's got a solution for climate change, okay? I've got to finish up here. I still need proteins." I was about to leave but his eyes were still shiny. "So you're okay, Benny? I'll see you back home?"

"You keep going, Barb. Proteins."

I squeezed his hand and set off. Deep down, Benny was with me on the important issues, when his appetite wasn't getting in the way.

I was headed for canned tuna when a deafening boom shook the building. The vibration lasted several seconds. People gasped and stopped. The lights went out. The scanner beeps stopped. One long and uneasy moment of quiet followed before people began murmuring and a voice called instructions I couldn't hear. Everyone started rushing through the darkness toward the exits, abandoning their carts. I couldn't leave mine. I was frantic, wheeling it down aisles, looking for Benny, to warn him about going outside into an unknown situation. The store was emptying. I breathed shallow gulps of air, pushing the cart, trying to fight the urge to join the panic and leave. I needed to calm down. Figure out a plan.

I saw the detergents. A place to hide and regroup until I understood the nature of the threat. I'd phone Benny and check in on Carson. I shifted enough boxes out to make space and crawled onto the shelf. I tried my phone but there was no reception. It was dark and silent. No music, scanner beeps, price checks. No messages for shoppers. The boxes around me like gravestones.

Soon I heard the squeak of rubber-soled shoes and a voice, as precious as my own heartbeat, calling my name.

I could only manage a whisper: "Benny."

"Barb!" He was near, then pulling the boxes out, and leaning into my hiding spot. "Honey, what are you doing? They want everyone outside. I snuck back in when I didn't see you."

"Carson! I have to call."

"I already did. June's helping him paint the piñata."

"He shouldn't be outside. It's not safe."

"Barb. It's not what you're thinking. It was just a delivery truck. It rammed into the building, knocked down some wires. Everything's okay."

"I'm so frightened. I can't stop worrying."

"Let's share the worrying. We can worry together."

I reached out to stroke his cheek and the lights flicked on, only dimly. A guitar solo began playing, a song I couldn't place.

"Hey, see? They have the generator going."

"Benny, only you would know to come find me here. Only you understand."

"This is good, Barb. We're really listening to one another, really talking." I stared at his face squeezed in between detergent boxes and wanted to laugh. Benny smiled. "We should celebrate tonight. Have a special dinner."

That reminded me. "The stew, though. What about all that energy consumption? I can't live with that."

"Okay, I'll barbecue instead. Beef kebabs. Mmm."

"Lower, Benny."

"Sausages?"

"*Lower.*"

"Okay, chicken. Forget tofu, Barb. There's no way I'm putting that stuff on the barbecue."

"All right, chicken."

"What do you say we have friends over?"

"You've already invited Joel."

"It'll be like when we were young. Like it used to be."

"That does sound kind of nice. Benny?"

"What is it, Barb?"

"I could really use a cuddle right now."

Cassandra eyes the clock. "It's probably getting busy. I'd better go."

Ron fast forwards until some guy is on his hands and knees with his head between the Ultra-Paks. The store lights are partly on, affording a better view of his wide bottom.

"Who's that?" She's interested again.

"Who knows?" They watch as two slender hands reach out and grasp the man's arms. He backs away, helping the woman out and up to standing. They converge in a tight clinch, their mouths locking together.

Cassandra stares at the monitor. "That's new."

"You can bet the dweebs in Marketing would never expect consumer behaviour like this. Does it really surprise you, though? Some people can't control themselves with the lights off." Ron slaps the arm of his chair and swivels to look at her. "Well, that had to be worth a trip up to my lair, eh? Care to climb on and join me for a little spin?"

Cassandra isn't listening. Why should she pay attention to someone who reads gaming magazines in a darkened room with no clue about what it's like down there. He doesn't know how easy it is to slip into a robotic trance slicing greasy meats in the fake sunshine. There are times she wants to escape the counter and run like that woman did. Or drag her hands down the perfect displays, start an avalanche of gum, oranges, potato chips. When the truck crashed and the power went out—in that moment when no one knew what to do—she felt a surge of excitement. Like the electricity was coursing through her instead of the store.

Cassandra opens the door. "Sorry, Ron. Gotta go. Gotta go serve the people."

When she hands over a tub of green coleslaw or bag of limp ham, she'll look for a flicker of recognition in their eyes, a hint that they're also thinking about how ridiculous things have become.

OH MARY, MAH-LEE,
MANDY

—

IT'S NOT OFTEN A FOREIGNER APPEARS in Mrs. Chin's thirty-eighth-floor apartment. I have the only blue eyes and blond hair in the neighbourhood and she's determined to show them off. Every morning before breakfast, she drags me down to the crowded street market and takes her time selecting from identical oranges heaped on carts so that my Caucasian features can be thoroughly inspected by the grinning fruit and vegetable hawkers. My insecurities shine like the layer of sweat on my skin. Then we pass the sidewalk butcher with the missing digits. At his feet, the severed head of an ox gives me a one-eyed get-over-it stare.

Two weeks into my trip and a few days left to endure. I have journeyed to this family of Chins—to their 550-square-foot sky-pad with bedrooms the size of beds. I had been content with my room in Mom's condo and job in her gift shop, with all that Canadiana bric-a-brac: loons on turquoise sweatshirts, scented CN Tower candles. Then came the call from Winnie Chin, Mom's Hong Kong–based supplier and good friend, inviting me to visit.

"Oh, Mary, go!" Mom had chimed. "It'll change your life." (That's what I'm afraid of.) "Maybe you'll meet someone special." (I'm afraid of that too.)

I was launched Far Eastward within the week.

Only to land in a city so frenzied it pains my brain to walk it. Sidewalks packed to elevator-density mere centimetres from highway-speed traffic, dangling signage poised to crush unsuspecting pedestrians, a constant soundtrack of jackhammers, the humid air a pungent brew of fish, diesel and musty herbs. Two days of that and I gave up on sightseeing, tried escaping to the malls on the advice of my *Broads Abroad Shopping Guide* (gift from Mom). Endless boutiques stocked with expressionless sales waifs but never jeans big enough for North American butts. I gave up on shopping too.

I'm eating Mrs. Chin's pork congee while she watches. I'd give anything for a bowl of cornflakes but, as Winnie explains, old Chinese people are against cold food. Which may be why my cereal box disappeared from the cupboard—fed, perhaps, to Mr. Chin's loosely chained feral dog on the roof terrace where I'm sent each morning to hang the laundry, certain the snarling mutt will break free and force me to leap out into empty air.

Winnie is always at work and I'm generally fabricating events for the postcards I send to Mom and hanging out with Mrs. Chin. Unfazed by our lack of a common language, she talks at book-length in Cantonese. I nod a lot. I nod when I guess her meaning. I nod when I'm tired of guessing. She bruises my arm, pulling me from room to room to show me what will surely invigorate her lethargic houseguest: a grimy window, a basket of dirty clothes. In response, I've started drawing again. The other day, she pushed me toward the apartment door, maybe thinking I should give sightseeing another go. I reached for paper and pencil and got to work. Ever try to illustrate a preference for the safety of the home front? A general fear of risk, both physical and emotional? By the time I produced the twenty-frame storyboard, she was busy in the kitchen. I tried to show her but she shook her head, chortling, then whacked a hunk of meat with a cleaver. The whole communication thing is exhausting but keeps me occupied.

Dinnertime and the humidity's getting me cranky as I help set out the steaming dishes. Grouper, bok choy, a new kind of meat. (The dog wasn't on the roof today so I won't be touching that one.)

Winnie, just back from work, fingers my new shirt: a front-buttoned polyester number with an abstract pattern in murky browns and purples and flecks of gold. "What is happen, Mary? You dress like old Chinese lady!"

Mrs. Chin sits down at the table and gives an approving nod. She bought this shirt for me on the way home from the market, slapping my hand when I tried to put it back. I gave in and wore it, unable to sketch the complex relationship between clothing and personal identity.

"What are you do today, Mary?"

Dear Winnie, still hopeful I will transform into a camera-carrying tourist. She flips through my stack of cartoons like a jaded critic.

"Maybe I shouldn't have come here. I don't travel well. I miss home." The truth was, I missed everything: the lilac outside my bedroom window, the CN Tower, even Parliament Hill—and I've never even been to Ottawa.

"You cannot yet go back with not *see* something." She points a chopstick at me. "Without *do* something. I promise to your mom you getting life *experience*."

"I did go shopping the other week."

"You buy socks! You not even come yesterday getting hair perm with me!" Her eyes bulge.

Mr. Chin shuffles over and pokes the mystery meat with chopsticks, then sits, his attention locking onto the TV and the Triad drama he watches nightly. Mrs. Chin is immersed in the pleasures of bok choy. Our English words are invisible speech bubbles hovering over the dinner. Winnie's got me discombobulated. I frown at the small cube of meat that has appeared in my bowl.

A dream of wild dogs that have just been to the salon—fur nicely coiffed, mouths foaming. Dream of a city, a frightening chessboard, all squares filled, a city with tropical air that makes everything limp, even cereal boxes.

My cereal box, taken from me.

I gasp awake to darkness and the mournful shriek of truck brakes far below. It's 5:01 a.m. There's a rapping at my door and then Mrs. Chin's plastic slippers shuffling by. Then *slap!* (Another cockroach flattened on the parquet.) Winnie told me about Mrs. Chin's daily pre-dawn walk on a mountain road with her buddies. There was some talk among the Chins, apparently, about exercise doing me some good. I peer out the window and can just make out part of the mountain's menacing silhouette beyond the buildings. I retreat under the covers. The front door shuts and she's gone.

The white eye of the steamed fish has a green-onion eyebrow. It is the target of Mr. Chin's chopsticks. Mrs. Chin selects a boneless chunk of flesh and plops it into my bowl. Beside me, mouth full of rice, Winnie is on a rant.

"You need meeting people, okay? This weekend your last one, okay? So tomorrow you join my friends at all-day boat party."

"On open water?"

"Mary. Is *safe* and *fun*."

"Maybe I could just watch from the shore. Or what if I stay here in the apartment and you check in with me every so often by cell?"

Winnie blurts out in Cantonese, keeps going on, and even Mr. Chin looks over. When he slams his fist to the table, something's been decided.

A knock at my door jolts me awake. It's 5:01 a.m. If I don't agree to this pre-dawn walk, I'm in for a full day trapped on a boat. I scramble for my sweats and polyester shirt and find Mrs. Chin waiting for me in the living room.

"Mah-lee!" Mrs. Chin squeezes my face between her hands. *"Jo san!"*

I grab sketch pad and pen as Mrs. Chin's withered hand, joints of steel, tugs me out to the hall and into the elevator. On the long ride down, she talks non-stop. Immersed in her perfume of mothballs and steamed rice, I watch her gesture widely in the tiny space. She could be complaining about Mr. Chin—seldom home, sullen when he is. She could be giving me the lowdown on the mountain walk. The elastic sounds of Cantonese stretch around and round my head.

Outside, the early-morning air is a warm, groggy hug. The sidewalks—hallelujah!—are empty. A few blocks and we arrive at the base of the mountain, where we face a significant incline. Right. A mountain walk is an *uphill* walk. Mrs. Chin charges ahead, catching up to a pack of old ladies with polyester shirts just like ours, and I'm left huffing in her wake. But I'm in the company of other cheerful seniors. Climbing and descending, they greet me, and one another, with mellow calls of *Jo san*.

Twenty minutes up and Mrs. Chin and friends veer off to a large plateau edged with trees. They form a loose circle and begin bending and stretching and chatting, their exclamations and rants mingling with birdsong. I haul myself over to a bench, avoiding the long view down. When I turn around, two newcomers have joined Mrs. Chin's clique: another old lady and, standing beside her, a man. An octopus of old arms waves me over.

He's decked out in black with slicked-back hair and looking out of place in this milieu—a probable son/nephew/unsuspecting-target-of-matchmaking. His cool demeanor just like that of the Triad thugs on Mr. Chin's TV show. He stands with hands in his front jeans pockets while Mrs. Chin and friends pelt him with Cantonese. They point at me, at him, at the sky, the earth and the trees I will soon eat if I don't get some breakfast, preferably cornflakes. Then everyone over the age of sixty shifts away, leaving the two of us stranded on the dirt.

He grimaces toward me. "Why you make frown? Is sunny day."

I squint upward.

"Why you hang round old ladies?"

"I'm just visiting. A tourist."

He gives me a head-to-toe scan.

"Okay. So I promise to them show you *exciting* of Hong Kong."

"Wait. That's not going to work. I'm not —"

"First, we go *yum cha*. Dim sum." He snaps his fingers like he's already impatient for the food to arrive.

I'm starved, true, but much safer to stick with Mrs. Chin

and whatever gristly meat-and-rice concoction is stewing back at home base. But his arm is around my shoulder and he's whisking me away, accompanied by a round of clapping from Mrs. Chin and friends. There's no time to sketch a protest. In fact, I've forgotten my sketching materials on a bench.

I'm chewing a tentacle in an underground restaurant. I learn that he learned English from Barry Manilow. He pours endless cups of leaf-strewn tea as dark as his secret world, slurps his meal, tosses tiny animal parts into my bowl, all the while surveying the room, attentive to potential dangers and also to the significant profile of his biceps in a nearby mirror. I consider this bizarre possibility: I might be safest hanging around this gangster.

Then, in a black Mercedes—with an excellent crash-test rating—it's a hair-raising hairpin ride on a mountain-hugging road. I check and my knuckles are still pink, a sign I won't faint. We park by a beach and take a stroll. We snack on sweet buns before zipping toward Kowloon in the under-harbour tunnel. A four-minute drive in artificial darkness. He cranks the stereo. Manilow croons.

He looks at me with eyes as dark and glistening as lychee pits. "How you like?" he asks.

"It's hard to take him seriously."

"Huh?"

"Barry."

"No. How you like so far exciting Hong Kong?"

"I'm terrified. But I think I like it." The air con, the leather seats. The comforts of his world offset the potential unknowns. I feel reckless, sort of.

He reaches across to touch the tip of my nose. "You strike me."

"If you mean striking, I'll take that as a compliment. I'm against violence." I understand, though, how it might be how things work in his world. My heart romps round my chest. "My name, by the way, is Mary."

He laughs because of the song that's playing and suddenly he's singing along. *"Oh Mandy, well you kiss me and stop me from shaky! And I need you today, oh Mandy!"*

"What's your name?" I ask, blushing. Everything's moving too quickly: his car, this date.

"I'm Pong." Then he points at my shirt. "This no good."

Despite my protests, we shop. At each store, he stands by the entrance with chest out, arms crossed. His presence makes me bold. I drop the polite tourist shtick, start insisting the diminutive clerks turn the place upside down looking for something that fits.

Late lunch in a noodle joint—I'm resplendent in a sequined blouse, embroidered butterflies in flight from right breast to left shoulder. It's a new look I'm working through. It came down to butterflies or the Bruce Lee-with-nunchucks T-shirt Pong picked out for me. Pong sucks up his meal in one extensive slurp. Then it's a whirling, swirling, twirling drive up into mountains. To the Peak, where we look down at the panorama of towering offices and apartments and harbour and more apartments strewn across the horizon. Countless lives in a sea of windows.

And what of my life? After this jam-packed day, I reflect on its skimpy plot line. Its recent lack of events. My fault for not getting back out there years ago after Dad took off, after Peppy ran into traffic, after my art teacher suggested I pursue accounting, after my first love found truer love with my best friend. My fault for not sucking it all up and diving back into the fray like you're supposed to when you're young and brave and stupid.

I turn to Pong. "We are young," I recite, remembering another old song. "Heartache to heartache we stand."

He checks his watch. "You want experiencing my true passion?"

New to the dating game, and it being still before dinnertime, I find this a bit forward. But goddamn, it's time to live!

"I might be able to handle a sampling."

He ruffles my hair and we Mercedes back down a quiet road and pull up to a tiny building surrounded by trees. From inside come blood-curdling shrieks. I come to my senses. Strange man. Gangster man. Secluded location. *Holy crap.*

Pong grips my arm and leads me to the door. Inside, a large, empty room and a group of people in loose black pants and T-shirts doing kung fu.

They stop and put their palms together and nod to him. He nods to them and pulls me in.

"New student," he says.

I am handed an outfit.

When I emerge from the dressing room, Pong is in a loose outfit too. I'm about to crack a little joke about pyjamas, lighten the mood, when he orders me to punch him. He tells me to scream when I punch. "From your gut," he says.

I extend my fist and tap at his stomach.

"No." His eyes bore into my forehead. "Do not bullshitting, Mandy. Show passion. From the gut."

Gut? I want to say: How much more gut can one woman show in a single day? But he's yelling at me—face contorted, unattractive—and I'm feeling those little animal bits from dim sum and the sweet buns all swirling around in my stomach and everyone's staring and my face is on fire but the challenge is there and I'm rising like the bile to meet it. I punch him as hard as I can.

"Impressing. You are stronger than you are thinking."

"Thank you," I say, and throw up on his feet.

Back at the Chin pad for dinner, I set three bowls on the table. (Winnie's on her cruise and won't be home until late.) Mr. Chin picks chicken from his teeth with the long nail of his baby finger, waiting for me to stop blocking the TV. The Triad show is on. From up on the roof, we hear barking. He grabs a plate of fatty meat and leaves the room. I switch the TV off and sit. Beside me, Mrs. Chin is staring at my butterfly shirt.

I want to tell her about my crazy day, about how brave I've been, especially in declining to sign up at Pong's School of Kung Fu and suffering his sudden lack of interest in me, and the wait afterwards at the lonely bus stop. I see my sketch pad on the couch and bring it over to the table, but somehow reporting on the day's events is not what I feel like doing. Still, my pencil hovers over the paper like it's determined I draw *something*, and when I look up I notice my reflection in the dark TV screen. It's more of a silhouette but I sketch it anyway and start filling in all the details from memory. I know my own pathetic face only too well. But my expression I make fierce, like I'm punching away everything scary and it's all from the gut, just like this drawing. Which is no cartoon. No, this is teetering toward something I might call art. I'd like to keep working on it and get it done before I head back home tomorrow. I'd like it to be good enough to give to Mom as a little thank-you for this trip.

Mrs. Chin shouts, "Mah-lee! Mah-lee! Mah-lee!" and when I look up she's pointing at my bowl of chicken and rice. Her face is wrinkled and serious and beautiful. She's telling me to leave the drawing for some other time and just pay attention to this poultry-scented moment.

NOTES FROM
THE FALLEN

THE PAMPHLET SHOWS A CARTOON penguin tipping backwards, about to slip on some ice. Blank circles for eyes, wings out looking for balance. *Falls are a serious concern for the elderly, accounting for 85% of hospital visits.* Then more statistics and supposedly helpful garbage. I'm thinking a fall might be *nice*. A fall into a better situation. A fall into another state of mind. Maybe even a fall into love. But the only falling around here is from old unsteady legs onto cold hard floors.

I rip the pamphlet into sixteen pieces and tuck them into my purse.

We sit randomly on the chairs along this straight hallway. Or we pace it, biding time until our minds are deemed stable enough to go home. Or to *a* home—the final frontier.

My niece brought me here again like an old beater in for repairs. First my prescription ran out, then laundry detergent, shampoo, food. She found me with scissors. Little heads cut from magazines scattered across the kitchen table. Just trying to find some pieces of mind. A ransom note *to* my brain *from* my brain. Several weeks of meds in a supervised setting and now I'm pretty much tuned up. I'm close to earning my exit papers. Daily chats with the Doctor to monitor my progress. *Fine, fine, fine, I'm fine.* Looks like a beautiful day out there. I wouldn't mind being out there in it. Not so great being locked up at the height of summer, windows screwed shut, air fetid. *Oh yeah, I am feeling just fucking fine. And how the fuck are you?*

We pose a danger to ourselves and/or others. Until our aged bodies absorb the right combo-pak of pharmaceuticals and counselling, we are stuck here together, a grubby grey herd. All we want, I think—haven't conducted a formal survey—is to be back in our own crappy apartments. All we want is decent food and a clean place to take a crap.

All we want is to get outside once in a while.

Out into the park right beside this very building.

But first we have to sort things out with the Doctor. It's important not to yell, not to be anti-social, not to act too happy, not to rush at people.

Bald Thomas sits beside me saying the sun will explode. Some kind of technical glitch he doesn't elaborate on. At any rate, just like us, it isn't functioning properly. Problems even at the cosmic level.

Julius passes by, listing sideways with each step. Hip issue. He travels the hallway back and forth, back and forth, but never out. From the dining room end to the end with the exit door—locked unless you earn a half-hour pass to the great outdoors. Or the grand prize: release papers. The exit door has a red sticker readable from the other side: *Warning—AWOL Risk.* On the wall near the door is the hand-sanitizer dispenser. Julius spreads the foam onto his forehead. What a nutbar. Then he heads toward the activity room—only unlocked during supervised "activation" events. The Scrabble boards and pencil crayons and adhesive tape and decks of cards safely secured. The scissors. Those too.

Here in the Leisure Room, it's just me and Mr. Klepto, freshly released from the Observation Room after filching everyone's eyeglasses and slippers a few days ago.

A video is playing. The Galapagos Islands. Pretty birds tinker around on the rocks. There's a turtle too. The size of it! Older than any of us. When I was young I wanted to go to the Galapagos. Sit on a rock. Feel perfect air smacking my face. If I'd gone, maybe I would have evolved into something better. Not ended up here.

The next part of the show is shot from a helicopter: water and islands. Is Mr. Klepto also loving this distraction from painted concrete walls? No. He is staring at my watch. *Watch out,* say his slowly blinking eyes. *Watch. Out.*

The painting bolted to the wall in the hallway is famous. It's coated with plastic so it can be spray cleaned. Julius presses his head to the field of sunflowers like he's trying to transfer all that beauty into his brain. Some days are just like that. Feeling around with curled fingers: ineffectual.

One of us fell hard, very hard. The one who was confused. She asked where she was, she watched my eyes for the answer. For the way out.

In the weeks beforehand I kept her company. She kept asking about her family. Over and over and over, I might add. I'd no sooner answer a question than the same one would roll right back at me. She had a husband, not well enough to visit, a daughter, a clear-headed sister. We found blank paper in her room and drew pictures of flowers—always a safe subject. She had trouble with her name. I printed it in pink crayon: Cora.

Sandra with the big yellow wig grins as she walks. She carries a notebook. I've peeked inside: neatly penned gibberish. Wacky stuff. Yet crazy Sandra gets half-hour outside passes. Later I'll see her through the window, sitting next to the garbage can and pulling bits of bread from lunch out of her pocket. Ignores the pigeons, will only feed sparrows.

To me the Doctor says: Not yet. I tell him summer's almost over and it would be nice if I could get out and enjoy it.

"All I want is one breath of fresh goddamn air. Is that so unreasonable? I'm sixty-six years old and you're young enough to be my kid! You don't know a bloody thing! You're nothing more than a third-rate, five-cent goddamn quack!"

I shouldn't have said that in the hallway. Not yelled when I said it.

Important to remember: when there's an incident, there's an Incident Report. Doesn't matter how well you *were* doing, an incident sets you back to square one. Fourteen days of clean behaviour to get a clean report. A clean report is what gets you out.

Yelling in the hallway. Questioning the Doctor's credentials. Calling everyone assholes. That's an incident. The nurses promised not to call in the goons if I calmed down. I calmed down.

I calmed down.

All I wanted was five minutes outside. Or a dull pair of scissors and a magazine. Consolation prize.

The nurses huddle in the office. I watch them through the glass. Shift change. Checking charts and discussing the latest incident, if it has been that kind of day. Code White, Code Blue, Code Red.

We're clustered in a herd outside the dining room. Waiting for lunch to be set up. Here in the hallway, Mr. Klepto has been installed in a chair with a snap-in tray. The tray is empty, save for his hands—empty hands. His face sad for that emptiness. I take one of the ripped-up pamphlet pieces from my purse and toss it onto the tray. Klepto doesn't even look up. He just lets the paper *be* there, the existential creep.

A nurse opens the door and we shuffle in. Our trays are set up with dessert and milk or juice, and the plastic cutlery—any self-inflicted wounds herewith shall be superficial. The whole event is one mad rush. The nurses want snappy eating so they can lock up and go check on the feeble ones stuck in their rooms.

The food is easy target for complaint. There are three distinct mounds: meat, veggie, starch. Words to describe it: crappy, disheartening, pathetic. Salt or nuanced flavour: absent. We leave our grey green beans untouched. At least there's always dessert. The cakes and puddings do not offend. Confused Cora used to aim her fork first at dessert. That, or put her hand in her soup. What do I do? she'd ask. *Use the spoon, put it in your mouth. What is it?* she'd ask. *Food.* You could laugh like Julius the shit-head or you could consider this: maybe one day you'll be living a nightmare like hers. Do your crossword puzzles with your fingers crossed.

Can't escape these sunny yellow walls. They smile as brightly as the Doctor as he chats with me. I think I sound pretty good, pretty with it, despite Cora's big fall the other day. The Tragedy.

Today at two the young Belinda will facilitate a discussion of "Life Skills." Attendance is encouraged by the Doctor. Therefore I'll be there with bells on. I'd go just to marvel at Belinda's youthful complexion: a wonder. Thomas will attempt to change its hue with smutty jokes.

At dinner Mr. Klepto pushes back from the table and stands, shrieking, his jaw rigid. He is wearing a gown, loose at the back. Nurses scramble to isolate him.

"Don't touch him," one barks.

As if we would, moron.

He is coaxed from the room. Still eating, we look or don't at his bare flat butt.

"They should have double-gowned him," Julius says. "Makes me fucking sick."

Sandra is across the table from Julius. That wig of hers is askew, grey wisps like cobwebs on her forehead. "I'm voluntary," she tells him. "I'm just here while things are worked out with my lease. I have two cats and my friend is watching them." Something from her fork drops into her tea. "This cake isn't bad. Have you tried it?"

"I see your mouth flapping," Julius says, "but I'm not listening. I'm trying to eat my fucking dinner."

I drink my tea, barely warm. Confused Cora once said hers tasted like smoke.

"I live with twins," Sandra says, "and they're called 'Anxiety' and 'Anger.' We're all terribly close."

We nod. Sounds reasonable enough. We're in the hallway waiting for bedtime.

"Remember 9/11?" Thomas asks her.

"Why?" she says.

"Alignment of the planets was out of whack."

Sandra's eyes find mine and widen. She's on the lookout for a confidante, a comrade, a coffee clutch. I'm not buying. I'm on the lookout for scissors, but I'd settle for a deck of cards and one hundred games of solitaire.

The radio comes on through the speakers. *Muskrat Love*, followed by a traffic report. Jack-knifed truck blocking all exits. Sandra slumps away, trailing a complex perfume of *Eau de Crotch* and fabric softener.

I look at my fellow passengers on this geriatric cruise through the mental-hell system and think: what have you lost, my dears, that brings you here? Because we have all lost something less obvious than willpower or our minds. The people who anchored us, perhaps, or the ability to distinguish a threat from an offer of help.

I spent time with Confused Cora in her room. She was mostly sweet. Prim smile, pinhead pupils in rheumy blue eyes. Child-like. Unless she mistook your helping hand for an attacking one, and reacted accordingly. She only hit me twice. I didn't take it personally. When she slapped Julius he raged for hours. She thought his room was hers and wanted the intruder out. That evening, her daughter came and stayed a long time. She and Cora's sister were often around, involved. Cora had one of the few private rooms in the unit. Windows looking into trees. In my room there's four of us. White curtains between beds. Like a really rotten sleepover we're way too old for. I'm not complaining, just observing what a hands-on family will land you. It's all about the squeaky wheel.

You wonder how you'll get through another brain-numbing day. Interminable morning, afternoon of piped-in radio, dinner of brown food, evening under ceiling fluorescents, fitful sleep, outbursts in the hallway. You hope you can do it. And somehow you do. Human adaptation: it's amazing.

Daughter of Confused Cora comes in through our exit door. Straight back, brisk pace. Sunglasses on, face puffy. I duck into the bathroom, peek out. Small suitcase in hand, she marches to Cora's room. Fascinating. It's not just the weight of each step, it's what she brings to our stale air: her relative youth and, floating in her wake, the sweet smell of summer.

Dear green leaves, I miss you all.

I was in Cora's room five days ago when it happened. I was telling her about the early years: Dad lost in his books in some corner of the house, Mom vacuuming the drapes again. Cora stretched her hand out to something. *Mom? Dad?* she called. There they were, right in front of her. Alive! Her parents, not mine. Finally come to save her from her nightmare. She lurched from the chair. Reaching out. Hands grasping to touch what her eyes believed. She fell hard, though. Right onto the tiled floor. Instead of a reunion, a brutal thud, then silence.

Then screaming. Mine, not hers. Next, commotion. Nurses, doctor, paramedics. She's rolled out on a stretcher. Dead the next day.

Well, it's all spelled out in the brochure.

"Life Skills" again in the Activity Room. Cookies and Styrofoam cups with urine-yellow apple juice. It's like playschool but you don't get hugged or picked up at the end.

We're brainstorming, though that's not—*ahem*—the term used, given the general prevalence of storms of the brain. It's more like we're discussing. Or Belinda's talking and we're putting our heads, our manic or delusional or substance-deprived heads, together to make a condolences card. We care. Even Julius is with us, though not on topic. He insists we buy a certain type of Vietnamese hot sauce that is virtually unavailable, though it's the only type worth using. He won't shut up about the bloody hot sauce as we pass the big card and add our name and a little decorative drawing of something benign, like Thomas's erupting volcano. Getting a card like this could scare a person to death.

Her family sent an azalea. Through the glass we admire the pink flowers where it sits on the desk in the staff office. Her room is already filled with a new admission. Always so many waiting on the lists, lists, lists.

Listen, I feel bad. But the main thing is, I'm counting my blessings. I've been managing okay since that woman cracked her head on the floor in front of me. And I'm counting five clean days since the sight of leaves and sky through the window made my brain implode. That makes nine more to go for a clean fourteen. I'm banking on getting through them. Nine days of bland benevolence. Nine days of keeping my balance.

I'm no fucking penguin. I can do this.

WALKING ALONG STEELES
AFTER MIDNIGHT

———

WE ARE SIX COURSES INTO Clarence Lau's wedding banquet up at the north edge of the city. Two courses left to go. A waiter moves from table to table pouring red wine. Another carries pitchers of Orange Crush and Coke.

Clarence and I work at an electronics store. So does Gordie, who is sitting beside me. Gordie and I are both married, but spouses weren't invited. Although I didn't really want to come tonight, the invitation had the weight of an obligation. The small talk at our table ran out before the meal started but shrill music blasting from the speakers is keeping things festive. We watch a slideshow on a screen beside the stage, a repeating loop of family members posed in various living rooms, images that make me want to get up and stretch, even walk right outside into the blizzard that started when I set out from our apartment downtown. Gordie's offered to give me a ride to the subway after the banquet. There aren't any windows in this

Chinese restaurant, so we don't know how bad things will be out there when it's time to leave.

Clarence and his bride come over to our table. He's holding a glass of wine and his face is also red. With his glasses off, his eyes look big and crazed. He says we should all have dim sum together soon, as if it's something we would do. His bride smiles at each of us. She hasn't stopped smiling all night. I remember my own wedding two years ago: feeling cushioned from uncertainty, and being surprised, too, that a decision Yousef and I made could result in so many people together in one room.

The next course arrives and we stay still while the waiter mechanically serves out portions of noodles on small white plates. The entertainment is Clarence's brother shouting into the mic in Cantonese, his voice hoarse and manic above the music and conversation. A Chinese man across the table tells Gordie and me that they're going to start playing games to embarrass the bride and groom. The waiter sets my plate down hard. Dotting the noodles are shiny, unusual mushrooms, round and black, like the buttons on my cardigan. I wore this cardigan even though it's really not dressy enough, because all I wanted was to be warm. When I was getting ready, Yousef had his head in the fridge, commenting about our food going bad all the time and the waste of it and how it directly related to our need to save every penny for our own place, which was important if we were going to start a family—which was our plan, right? As if my going out was spoiling both the food and our chance of conceiving. I said it was just pork chops I forgot to cook because they were hidden behind some beers. He turned to me and said my sweater looked too dowdy for a banquet, a lousy way of saying he wished I would stay home and help him figure out what to have for dinner. I said dowdy was the effect I was going for, and left.

The mushroom is slippery in my mouth. I look up while

I chew to distract myself from the texture and notice the short young man with surprised eyes who is walking along the wall of the restaurant. He's been doing this all evening, circling the room as if he'll eventually end up somewhere different. Nobody pays attention to him. I guess he's somebody's relative and is always like this. Every so often he stops and stares at the rows of lights on the ceiling, like he's charging up on energy, then he starts going around again. He is strangely free while the rest of us stay put, sitting and eating like we're supposed to. Stuck with these mushrooms and noodles that slip from chopsticks.

An amplified voice grabs our attention as the wedding party ushers the bride and groom onto the stage. Two bridesmaids dab white powder onto the bride's eyebrows. The best man turns Clarence to face his new wife and then she leans toward him until their noses touch. She swishes her face back and forth against his. It looks like they're kissing and people laugh. When she pulls away, the couple turn to present themselves to the large room full of guests. Clarence's eyebrows are now powdered white as well. The bridesmaids clap and the rest of the wedding party cheers. A woman at our table shouts across to me: "You understand? This means they grow old together! Good luck for their marriage!"

As soon as dessert is over, people get up fast to leave. The wedding party forms a line by the door and we shake hands one by one and say thank you. There's a lot of smiling. It went well and now it's over and everyone can go home and sleep.

Outside, the cars are mounded with hours of heavy snow. Under the sodium lights, they look like orange igloos. Gordie gets in his Honda and starts the engine. I stand and wait. The air stings my cheeks and I like it and the snow is still falling, but in a relaxed way after the storm's frenzy. When he comes back out and begins wiping the snow off, I realize I don't want to get in the car. I don't want to hear any more about Gordie's big plan to open a computer-repair business really soon. I don't want to hear anything. What I want is to be alone in this quiet and to walk. I want to cross the parking lot and walk along Steeles Avenue past closed stores and sleeping houses. Yousef will be asleep, too, his own private knot of concerns loosened by the startling world of his dreams, that part of him I'll never get to meet. Once, I asked him how he can be so sure about all the things we should do and he said it's like our deciding to get married, as simple as our warm fingers threaded together. While Yousef sleeps and dreams, I'll walk. I'll exhale cold clouds of air, a cloud for each of my doubts. Like whether I could get all the way home before he wakes, if home is where I head toward.

Gordie finishes wiping the snow off the car and I clear my throat. "Actually," I say, "I'd like to take the bus instead." The snow is a blanket pressing the air out of my voice, making it sound like it's been pre-recorded. If I mention walking, he'll probably say something to ruin the idea.

Gordie stares, his eyelashes thick with snowflakes. "What are you talking about? Get in, it's freezing."

I look toward Steeles Avenue. A car passes. The houses beyond are identical, all dark. Something familiar that's turned sinister, like a Christmas tree at night with the lights unplugged. Six years ago, I answered an ad for an office assistant at Gold Tech Electronics with the thought *Only until I find something better*. I'm still there, thinking about leaving, but doing nothing to make it happen. I keep showing up where I'm expected. Showing up to work and to weddings. Showing up at home.

I walk over to the Honda as if I've changed my mind, but I haven't. I want to feel my boots sink into thick new snow on a deserted suburban sidewalk. I've got my hand on the door and the snow is landing lightly on my face. It's just a matter of how to refuse the ride.

A LITTLE NUT THING

———

BENNY WAS HOME FROM ULTRA-STORE. He lifted a large box from the car, carried it up the front steps and plunked it down beside me in the hallway. He'd bought a laser printer but looked more like he'd won a prize. Beaming, he coasted back out to get the food I'd sent him to buy.

"You'll never guess what Huang said," I began when he was finally inside.

Crouched on the floor, Benny was poised to slice through the packing tape with the car key. A roll of flesh peeped out above his jeans.

"Who's Hong?"

"*Huang.* Huang who lives behind us. Cecelia's husband Huang with the reflective sunglasses I want to poke my finger through." Benny was listening but his expression was blank. "Huang who loaned you his snow blower last winter."

"That's his name? Nice guy."

"Wrong, Benny. He's an asshole."

"Barb, c'mon." He tilted his head sideways to read something on the box.

"What else would you call a person who would butcher a mature tree because it drops things?" I asked.

"What things?"

"Chestnuts. Our tree is dropping chestnuts into his pool. Now that pool season ends in late October, it overlaps with chestnut season. Because of climate change. He's complained before about the mess, but today he was going on about safety. They're having a kids' Halloween swimming party this weekend—if you can imagine something as asinine as waterproof costumes—and he's saying someone might get conked on the head and *drown*."

Benny snorted. "Sure, those things are spiky—but they wouldn't kill you." He turned the box around to read the other side.

"We already have a printer, Benny."

"This one is better. Only problem is..." He traced his finger across the small blue words and frowned. "It's not compatible with our operating system. Damn, it was such a good deal." He reached into one of the grocery bags, pulled out a package of Halloween candy and tore it open.

Our horse chestnut, *Aesculus hippocastanum*, is a splendid and healthy tree, as tall as the neighbourhood houses. Its canopy of broad palmate leaves provides shade for us and habitat for wildlife. Its regal display of scented white flowers awes us each June. The trunk is eleven inches in diameter and a leaf's length from our back fence. The fence is five and a half feet high, preventing visual contact with Cecelia and Huang and their pink-festooned progeny—seven-year-old twins Felicia and Stacia—

but does nothing to buffer the soundtrack of their boisterous pool-centric lives. The tree had been presenting problems for them since they built their house two years before, or so Huang claimed at every opportunity.

Earlier in the day, I'd been harvesting tomatoes when Huang and Cecelia called out. I had to stand on a bucket beside the fence to see over. Their chit-chat quickly segued to the topic foremost on their minds. There we were, three disembodied heads with Huang starting in on his death-by-chestnut theory. It's not like I'd been sitting around waiting for something to deal with. Life was lobbing everything my way: Benny's hockey-equipment store was being squeezed dry by big-box retailers, I was busy on the internet tracking humanity's descent into environmental hell while implementing a 100-mile diet and trying to finish sewing us one-piece polar fleece outfits (we'd keep the thermostat low to conserve energy in winter and at the same time be prepared for power outages), and Carson, our twelve-year-old, was being sued by a clothing manufacturer for libel related to his Kids Monitoring Kids' Rights in the Developing World blog. He'd also recently purchased a chinchilla without our permission and named it Gandhi. Huang's complaint about our tree threatened to send me over the edge.

Staring at my neighbours' heads, I attempted a philosophical approach. "Are trees," I began, "truly 'messy,' Huang, or could it be that your standards for the natural world are pretty unreasonable? Trees drop fruit for a purpose, right? If these life-giving items land in, say, a swimming pool instead of onto nutrient-rich soil, whose fault is that?"

He nodded as if agreeing, but his lips remained flat. Hidden behind the reflective shades, his eyes were unreadable. A thick wedge of hair dangled over his unperturbed forehead. He was a tall, meaty guy, almost the size of a fridge. Cecelia, also tall but more floor-lamp proportioned—thin with a mop of coiffed blond hair—stood squinting first at me, then at the horse chestnut, and then down to where I imagined their yippy Jack Russell to be either humping her shin or devising a new way to get into my garden.

Finally Huang spoke in precisely articulated English: "Basically, these chestnut fucking up our pool filtration system. What I going to do, Barb, is removing every branch hangs over my property. This is within my right and basically why I telling you is giving you the head up as one neighbours to another neighbours. And, hey, let us not allow this getting personal." His lips flattened again.

I couldn't remember exactly what he did for a living—something financial for a mega-corporation—but knew I was being treated to the hard-ass talk he likely doled out at work.

"If you do this, Huang, you will be butchering my tree. It will be *unbalanced*"—I emphasized the word as if it was an obscure technical term—"making it structurally unsound. Lopping off half a tree is a really, really crappy idea."

"So let us take the whole damn thing down and I will covering the cost. Basically, I willing to do that."

Cecelia turned and looked at the side of her husband's head. "Huang has tons of buddies who are *super* athletic. They're eager to help."

"This tree," I said, "comes down over my dead body. Basically."

Huang blew air through his lips. "I want no one gets hurt in this operation," he said. "Very complicating."

Anger rendered me speechless as Cecelia threw back her head and glared up at our glorious tree.

"You're really charged up about this tree business," Benny said. He was marching toward the back of the yard, hammock in hand, as I followed. "I worry it's going to get you going."

I shook my head as he unfolded the hammock. "This is serious, Benny. There's the tree, fine, but then there's what the tree *represents*. This is man—or, arguably, idiot—against nature." I glanced toward the multi-gabled roof of Huang and Cecelia's stucco palace. Or was it lifestyle against nature? "Don't you see the danger this precedent would set? If one tree goes in the name of ecologically ignorant tidiness, then—"

"A tree needs pruning. It's about a ladder and power tools. I looked at the situation. They don't have to take off nearly as much as they're saying. A few minor branches is all."

"Good god, Benny! You're so Problem Solving 101." He hooked the hammock to a fence post and was tying the other end around the trunk of the chestnut tree. "Huang's real agenda is to rip the whole tree down because it bugs his ass that something's rivalling the size of his big flipping house. But fine, you go talk to your buddy, Mr. Snow Blower. See how far you get."

"Right after my siesta."

A succession of splashes and little-girl squeals issued from the next yard, as Carson appeared at the back door. "I can't find Gandhi's raisins," he called out.

"On the fridge. But don't overfeed him." I turned back to Benny. "The last thing I need is an obese animal in my house."

"Hey, Barb, have you ever touched the fur of that little guy? Unbelievably soft." Benny's luxuriant sigh as he sank into the mesh fabric was accompanied by the crinkling of the mini-chocolate-bar wrappers scrunched into his pockets. "Did you know," he added, "that *chinchillas lack the ability to sweat?*"

I contemplated the deliciousness of lying in a hammock, something Benny made time to do with household tasks piling up and his business sputtering. I looked around at the chestnuts and their broken spiky green capsules scattered across the lawn and considered hurling a handful in the general direction of Huang and his brood. But, of course, that would only have fuelled their argument. I kicked one across the grass and headed back inside to finish sewing the fleece outfits.

That night I woke in the dark. Lying there, window open to the warm—unseasonably warm—fall night, I fretted about what Huang might do to our tree. With Halloween days away, he could act at any time. I needed to act first—but how? Strap myself to one of the threatened branches? I could hear Gandhi making chinchilla noises in the spare bedroom, whether crying or pontificating—*"Be the change you want to see in the world!"*—but at any rate sounding like a water-filled squeezie toy while he paced his cage. After a while he shut up, and I listened to the hum of traffic that trolled the Danforth every hour of every day. Trucks moving things from one end of the city to the other, taxis pacing the asphalt. The unrelenting depletion of non-renewable fossil fuels. I couldn't sleep.

I crept downstairs for a glass of water and stepped out into the garden. There was our tree, a silent, still shadow against the glow of light-polluted clouds and yet so entirely alive. And regal. And stoic. Tolerating whatever conditions it faced: droughts, excessive heat, sudden temperature shifts, ever-crazier storms. And the tree adapted, continued growing—what other choice was there? I shivered as the chill of night caught up with me. I looked up at Carson's bedroom window and tried to picture the world of his future—but couldn't go there. What I could deal with was keeping things status quo. As long as the tree was okay, maybe we'd stay okay.

The next morning, Benny and I sat out back drinking coffee and listening to the commotion in Huang and Cecelia's yard: unfamiliar voices issuing instructions, a motor starting up.

Preparations for the twins' party, no doubt. I worried about how Huang planned to handle the threat of death by falling chestnuts. How soon would his friends have a go at my tree?

I spent the rest of the morning canning our tomatoes. In the afternoon, Benny came swinging into the house.

"We're invited!" he shouted, already rummaging through the fridge. I could hear the unmistakable clinking of amber bottles. "To the Wangs' backyard," he continued. "It'll be a blast. A swimming pool still open at the end of October, for heaven's sake! How many more amazing days like this will there be this year?"

"For the planet's sake not many, I hope. It'd be good for autumn to kick in sometime before Christmas but—c'mon, Benny!—you can't possibly be serious about socializing with them."

"Something funny too: they rented a bouncy castle for the twins' Halloween party. It's actually a bouncy *haunted house!* The party's tomorrow but there was a screw-up and it came a day early, so Huang's letting the neighbourhood kids jump around in it. Everyone on the block's heading over. Crazy, eh?" Benny was loading the beers into a bag. "Huang is a riot! He rode down the sidewalk on Felicia's Barbie bike inviting everyone. He looked hilarious, like an elephant on that little thing. I bumped into him when he was pedalling back."

I was having trouble picturing this wild side of dour Mr. Huang Wang. "And so you've talked over your pruning idea?" I asked as he hurried to the front door.

"Later, Barb. You see my approach? Beers, some socializing, then I point to the tree and say: *Hey, Huang: blah, blah, blah.*" With his hand on the doorknob, Benny was smiling like he was touching the portal to a perfect parallel universe.

Two hours later, I was in the hammock staring up at the tree. From the other side of the fence, I heard music, splashing, boozy exclamations and Benny's whistling laugh—the one that develops after a few beers and sounds like he's out of air and about to keel over, a laugh that makes everyone else laugh. There must have been fifty people over there. The bouncy castle's motor hummed in the background. Lying there, I asked myself: why resist cultural indulgence if, as it did seem, the world's problems are probably too complex to solve? Maybe Benny had a point: enjoy the good times while they last.

Carson came across the lawn toward me. He'd spent a frantic afternoon scouring the house, trying to simulate the thought process of a chinchilla: Gandhi's cage door was open and the little sucker was missing. Carson had gone on Wikipedia to research its habitat preferences and behaviour—something he should have done before getting it from the Chinchilla Rescue Centre.

"Do you think I overdo it a little, Carson?" I mused aloud.

"Mom, I'm worried about Gandhi. What if he's hurt? Or sick? Or—"

"I bet Gandhi just took advantage of the open cage to find a new place to nap. He'll show up when it's dark and he needs to eat. Assuming he's not on a hunger strike." Carson suddenly looked about five years old. "Sorry, honey. He'll surface, don't worry."

"You just gave me an idea! I'll sprinkle raisins all over the kitchen and lure him out."

He was turning to run back when a chorus of laughter sailed over the fence and a deep voice yelled: "I've torn my wings, people!" I hadn't realized the adults were in costume.

Carson stopped. "Why aren't *you* over there with everyone, Mom?" He studied me the way kids do when alarmed by the realization their parent is not only flawed but possibly weird as well.

"Ahhhhh. Ethical dilemma, Carson. You know I feel strongly about protecting the environment. You're the same about your own causes, right? But what if someone with an unconscionable lifestyle—someone who is threatening to kill a healthy tree—invites you to their high-carbon-emitting party and you find yourself thinking, after some soul-searching, *why the hell not?*"

"Wow," Carson said. "So, you mean sometimes it's more like: *don't* be the change you want to see in the world?"

"Well, everybody needs a laugh now and then, right?"

"Maybe you can convince them not to wreck the tree while they're in a good mood," Carson said before running back into the house.

I gripped the sides of the hammock. Daylight was waning and the sky radiated a peculiar, pretty, greenish hue. A breeze rustling the dry leaves of the horse chestnut tree sounded like a deck of cards being shuffled.

Benny's head appeared over the fence. He wore a tiny pirate hat. "Barb! What are you doing still over there?"

I uncrossed my arms, laced my fingers behind my head. "Relaxing."

"You wouldn't believe their garden shed. Mini-fridge, ice crusher, *cappuccino machine*! It even has a bar counter lined with teeny-weeny sparkly lights. It's like a *resort!*"

"Check the dial on their hydro-electric meter. It's probably spinning at the speed of light."

"Come over, then. You can tell Huang about the solar panels you've ordered. Come on, Barbie-buns, we're starting another round of shots."

"How drunk *are* you, Benny?"

"Wait, I want to show you something."

His head disappeared and then a few feet away two fence

boards popped onto the grass. Benny's head appeared through the gap. "A shortcut. I've been meaning to fix those for a while." He looked over his shoulder. "Listen, I've got to go!"

Lying there alone in the gloomy dusk, I felt a sudden jolt of pain on my stomach. A fallen chestnut. Damn thing hurt more than I'd have thought. I peeled off the spiky flesh and pocketed the smooth nut. Now I was angry. Angry with Huang for partying so lightheartedly after threatening my tree, for inviting my husband and mollifying him with booze. If Benny wasn't going to deal with him, then I sure as hell was.

I squeezed through the fence and into a backyard as bright as a film set. Neighbours were variously draped on patio furniture by the pool, sidled up to the shed bar, playing poker, clumped beside the hydrangeas and trickling into the enormous orange and black bouncy castle that, jiggling and humming, took up half the lawn. The kids, already bored of the thing, were just inside the house, heaped on a Tetris-like arrangement of sectional sofas before the glow of a gigantic TV.

"Barb!" Cecelia shuffled over in a red wig, bikini top and silvery fabric that was unravelling from around her thighs. The Little Mermaid was my guess. She gripped the neck of a Grand Marnier bottle and handed me a plastic cup. She poured like it was pop. "This weather frigging rocks!" she said. "Cheers!" As I took a sip, her elbow banged my cup and sent the alcohol burning down my throat.

"Enjoy it now, folks," someone yelled. "Cold front's on the way. There'll be a storm tonight."

Cecelia raised the bottle skyward. "I love storms! They're so cozy." Then she froze. "Shit. What about the girls' Halloween party tomorrow?"

"Just rent a couple of those big propane heaters," I said, voice hoarse but unable to resist. "Just keep pretending it's July."

Cecelia tapped her bottle to my cup and headed toward the poker game.

I wandered to the back of the garden beside the pool with a plan to dump the rest of my drink. I was also curious to see how far the branches really did extend over the water.

"Coming over to looking at your tree?" a voice whispered in my ear. "You are very serious little woman." It was Huang, sunglasses off, his gaze mellower than I'd thought possible. "You really liking that tree, huh?" he asked. He stood close enough for me to smell the spice of his cologne, to hear the mighty exhalation of his colossal chest. My face burned. I pulled the chestnut from my pocket and handed it to him. A little smooth brown lump—a potential tree—rested in his open palm, dwarfed by it.

"I dunno," Huang said dreamily, "I dunno." The swimming pool shimmered in his eyes. I gulped some Grand Marnier. "This little thing. This little...nut thing."

"It's a chestnut." The tenderness in my voice surprised me. He stroked the chestnut's lustrous surface with his thumb as we both admired it.

"It is just..." Huang paused, then smiled and slipped it into his pocket. Placing his huge paw on my shoulder, he gazed up at the tree and so did I. Its sturdy branches were still thick with leaves. In the near darkness it appeared stately and mysterious. "It is just...troublesome to my family."

"When it flowers, though! You've got to admit—"

"Quite impressing, it is true."

I glanced from Huang to the bouncy castle and saw Benny slip inside. It was like I was in some strange art video. I looked back at Huang. What did I hope for here? A shift in perspective? For him to pledge that he would protect not only this tree but all trees from harm? Or to suggest that we harvest a bit of bark and some leaves, as they did in ancient China, to make a medicinal tea to share with the neighbours? Did I expect him to burst open like a capsule, his spiky outer layer falling away to reveal a rich inner core? The Grand Marnier was gaining control.

Suddenly Huang's voice cracked the air. "So unusual!" he shouted, stepping toward the fence.

"What is?"

"That squirrel. The sizes of its ears!" He pointed to a furry grey creature clinging to a low branch of the chestnut.

"Jesus," I said, "it's Gandhi!"

"It is type of squirrel?"

"Carson's pet!" I shrieked. "It might fall!"

Benny came up behind me. "Chinchillas can jump up to five feet at a go. But it's true they're not tree animals." He wrapped his arms around my waist, rested his chin on my shoulder. "Must have taken two, maybe three leaps to get that high. *Hold on, little guy!*"

"Let me handling this!" Huang said, hoisting himself up onto the fence. Surprisingly lithe for a man of his size, he grabbed at a branch near to the now-shrieking Gandhi and swung his legs up. "Listen!" he yelled down. "It is crying for expression of its own nature!"

I was struck with amazement. Seeing Huang up there in the tree. Realizing I'd never actually climbed it myself. Even as the situation got more complicated, it felt like things were getting better, more hopeful.

Huang thrust his hand out toward Gandhi, and from out of nowhere, the wind picked up. Furious gusts sent the branches swishing and dipping and swaying, sent leaves flying. A shudder of chestnuts plopped into the pool. Candy wrappers sailed by. It was like we were in an enormous blender. Everyone stopped carousing—everyone, that is, but the diehards inside the castle who kept on shouting "Whoa!" in unison as they jumped and jumped and jumped. They missed what was coming. They missed wildly gesturing flora, leaves smacking faces, chairs skidding across the patio and Cecelia screaming—things weren't looking so cozy after all. They missed the Wangs' wind chime tinkling spasmodically, unable to put a tune to the frenzy. The jolly bouncers missed the chestnut's offending branches snapping and plunging and us bolting for the house and Huang still up there in the tree, powerful and unfazed, holding on to the trunk with one arm, the other stretching out to the branch where Gandhi clung. They missed Huang's every muscle straining as he reached out to the helpless creature, almost within his grasp.

THE CHAIRS IN BJORN'S LIVING ROOM

JANIS ARRIVED AT BJORN O'REILLY'S live/work loft expecting a knock at the ten-foot-high door to produce a tall person. Face-to-face with her instead was a short man with a goatee and wavy black hair smoothed up off his forehead. She had seen him around since starting work downstairs at Tree Action Plan. Like many men in the building, Bjorn wore dark clothes and a solemn expression. But what set him apart were his moist copper-brown eyes. They suggested sensitivity and warmth. They also widened at the sight of her, as though her unexpected arrival presented a problem.

She introduced herself and handed him the espresso Kayla made her bring. Distracted by a crescendo of repeating piano chords coming from the loft, she stumbled through her request to print a map on his large-format printer. He accepted the USB key and led her through a long room past bookshelves and bare white walls that ended with a stellar view of the

Toronto skyline. It was February. The city looked cold enough to crack apart.

Janis's dream of becoming a forest ranger—walking on soft ground, breathing pure air—had brought her here from a small town carved out of the woods. But the dry science and heavy workload in first-year Forestry had proven too stressful. She had just dropped out when she met Kayla, who was taping up a poster that read "Save the Campus Tulip Tree." Mature tulip trees being rare, Janis had asked how she could help, and Kayla offered her a short-term job. Janis accepted, eager for a big-city experience before her apartment lease ran out and she was forced to return home to her family and to Gary and his 4x4.

Bjorn silenced the piano music with a remote. He pointed his goatee toward the living room and invited her to sit, then disappeared through a doorway. Janis looked at the furniture: eight different chairs made variously of pale woods, metal, beige leather and white plastic arranged in two rows on opposite sides of a red carpet, like malformed teeth around a furry tongue. One of the chairs resembled a squished plastic sphere. Another was a piece of burnished steel balanced on three pointed legs. Bjorn's living room lacked one standard item: a couch.

The printer started screeching and Bjorn emerged, holding the espresso at his trim stomach.

"It'll take a few minutes," he said.

"It's hard to know which chair to choose," she said, still standing.

He strode across the rug as if a switch had flicked on in his mind. "Each piece represents a decade in twentieth-century furniture. Well, at the moment starting with the 1930s—I'm still sourcing a Breuer for the '20s. And possibly a Macintosh for the previous decade—though that might involve shipping." Finally, he looked at her. "This is my collection."

The only thing Janis had collected was owls. Over the years, she'd amassed figurines, woodcarvings and even fridge magnets. But nothing this serious.

"The 1930s chair is a Corbusier. Like a minuet, simple yet intricate. This one is by Charles and Ray Eames: a pioneering use of bent plywood in the '40s." He told her the squished plastic one was called "Armchair 4794." He slid his hand along the curved wood boards of another, explaining how it represented hockey sticks, proving, he declared, that "furniture can reference revered cultural institutions." Airborne particles of his saliva glistened in the sunlight as he went on about "didactic tendencies" and "spatial integrity." It was as if Bjorn was in a separate room with his ideas and broadcasting them out to her like vital news items. She was amazed that a person could take a point of view and turn it into something you sit on.

Bjorn approached the last chair. It was entirely wood and remarkably plain. It looked like a hundred others Janis had seen in libraries and cafeterias.

"And this one," he said, sweat dotting his brow, "represents the current decade. It's mine."

"Aren't they all yours?" she asked.

"What I mean is I *designed* it. I design chairs. I'm an architect, but furniture is my adopted vocation. Passion, actually. I'm calling this the 'One Chair,' my first piece to go into production. This is the prototype. Hand-made. One of a kind."

"I like it." Janis scoured her brain for something to add. "It's simple—but I think that's good."

Bjorn plucked a small white towel from a shelf and pressed it to his forehead. "Simplicity. That was my objective. Relief from life's complexity."

The printer stopped and the abrupt quiet made Janis conscious of being alone with an attractive man. She was almost afraid to speak but remembered the Tree Action party they were hosting Friday to launch a new campaign and Kayla's instruction to invite Bjorn and borrow his black vinyl tablecloths. He gave them to her in a bag, sliding it onto her arm because her hands were full with the maps he'd printed. It was her first physical contact with a guy since leaving Minden.

"Parties," he said, "can be...uncomfortable." He touched the towel now draped around his neck.

"It's something about the noise," she said. "Or the crowding." Bjorn's eyebrows shot up. "Yes. *Both.*" He was staring at her as though she had just now appeared before him.

"But this party is important," she said. "The tree campaign needs everyone's support."

Bjorn's gentle smile lifted her through the doorway and all the way down the stairs, which she took two at a time, each slap of shoe against concrete like an exclamation of delight.

Janis sipped the first espresso she had ever tried. Kayla slid the open design magazine across the table toward her.

"Speak of the devil," Kayla said. With a pencil, she tapped a small headshot of Bjorn, leaving a mole-like dot between his eyebrows. The caption read: "O'Reilly chair to be distributed by Repose Furnishings."

Janis lowered her face to examine that lustrous dark hair, those copper-brown eyes. "He doesn't look like a Bjorn."

"His parents are from Dublin. They're graphic designers. They named him after some Danish designer they were obsessed with. And then he ends up obsessed with design."

Janis bit the edge of her paper cup. Bjorn's interest in chairs could be better described as expertise, an expertise he'd cleverly developed into a career. And that impressed her. Too many guys—Gary, for example—never followed through with plans, if they even had any to begin with. Janis reached for Kayla's pencil and erased the mark.

The loft filled with people Janis didn't know. Kayla was discussing how to prepare something called pad Thai with the only Tree Action person Janis recognized, and Kayla's brother, who was stoned and kept calling her a Northern Goddess, needed to be avoided. The music was a pounding cardiac beat with shrieking vocals. Everyone had to lean in close to talk, as if they were tasting one another's hair. Clearly, the tree campaign was not the evening's focus.

She sipped her cooler, faking nonchalance, until a voice reached her through the music.

"Kayla says you don't know anyone."

She turned to see Bjorn just as a song with a faster beat began. "I'm not from Toronto," she said, leaning toward him. "I'm from Minden." She put her hand to her shirt, as though to a badge for her hometown. Bjorn nodded gravely and motioned for her to sit before settling on the seat beside hers.

Kayla had told her that Bjorn was single but maybe not over a recent break-up with Yumi, a conceptual artist who travelled internationally to show her work—which had even involved shipping ferrets. Janis had been out of the country once, to Buffalo, when she was twelve. Kayla had said Yumi was serious and really into her work. What she hadn't needed to say was how that would make Yumi a perfect match for Bjorn. If he had loved a Yumi, what would interest him in a Janis?

"I keep thinking about chairs since you told me about them," Janis said. "They're more complicated than I'd thought possible."

"And since we spend so much of our time on them," Bjorn added, "you could say that our closest physical relationships are with chairs. So it isn't just about looks — it's about comfort, durability, reliability. A good chair should stay with you for life."

Perhaps it was the haze of alcohol, but Janis thought that was an odd way to talk about inanimate objects. She nervously bobbed her leg, an old habit, and in one fluid movement Bjorn pressed her knee still and withdrew his hand.

"Are you going to the Gutenmeyer after this?" he asked.

"I might," she said, "if I knew what it was."

"A gallery. Just west of here. There's an opening." He paused. "What's your background, anyway?"

"Family?"

"Professional."

"Oh. Forestry. Briefly. I mean, I love trees. Somehow it didn't work out. I'm kind of in limbo."

He drank some wine and raised a finger to signal a point coming. "Wood is something I'm into. Especially wood grain. I'm fascinated by its intricacy."

At first it sounded like he'd said "intimacy" and Janis wondered if he hadn't been hearing her properly either. The music was driving her nuts.

"About this opening," Janis began. "Can anyone go? I wouldn't mind leaving."

Bjorn studied her a moment before draining his wine. At the door, he donned a sleek black jacket. Janis plunged an arm into her teal parka. The Gutenmeyer sounded like a place where people were punished, but she looked forward to something new, something she wouldn't have known about if it hadn't been for Bjorn.

Bjorn waited with Janis on the sidewalk. Her streetcar had come into view. She wanted to talk some more but was at a loss about what they'd just seen: preserved, half-eaten dinners balanced on pedestals throughout the gallery. The atmosphere had been funereal and they didn't stay long because Bjorn had to get back to work.

"Do you like that kind of art?" Janis asked.

"I question his methodology. I mean, if you want to explore avarice and decay, there are other sources to draw from."

Janis was inclined to believe that landscapes and people made better subjects for art. In high school, Mrs. Walker had introduced her to classical painting and sculpture. She'd barely mentioned contemporary art. The final assignment had been to sketch a favourite place. She'd chosen the spot by Scott's Dam where the hemlocks jut over the river. Gary followed her down, though. She'd tried to concentrate on the texture of the trees while he licked her ear and worked his fingers into her underwear.

The resulting drawing, which she'd tried to fix later at home, brought her marks down.

As the streetcar glided nearer, Janis watched Bjorn's breath puff into the frigid air, a series of disappearing clouds.

"Maybe we could do this again," she said. "See more art or something."

"It's difficult to get away from my work. But I've enjoyed talking to you." He hugged her, pinning her arms. Janis was left uncertain if something had just ended or begun.

After work, Janis lingered in the lobby, reading the notice board with feigned interest. When the elevator opened Bjornless for the fifth time, she headed outside. She ignored the approaching streetcar and kept walking. Piled along the sidewalk was last week's snow, a miniature mountain range with blackened peaks that made her miss the hemlocks on the hills around Minden. Her mother had called the night before, asking her to come home. *Why do you want to stay in Toronto all alone? What are you doing with all that free time?* Watching TV and eating from packages, she'd wanted to say. Walking a lot. Thinking about a guy named Bjorn with a passion for chairs.

YES, MEAN CITY. These words printed on a storefront window stopped her. Mounted inside was a tiny painting: a row of old brick houses partly hidden by bare tree branches. She reached for the door. A woman with an afro sat at a laptop at the back of the room. Small canvases lined three walls, winter scenes of run-down buildings and alleys, the gritty parts of Toronto Janis found ugly. But the artist had intensified the colours, giving the scenes a surprising beauty. She moved from canvas to canvas, enjoying the many details of peeling store signs, puny street trees, sagging telephone lines. Beside the door were stacks of postcards for other shows. A name in bold green letters caught her eye and she picked it up: *"Yumi Watanabe—Body to City/Contact."* The show was opening soon at a different gallery nearby.

"I'm so looking forward to that," the woman said from across the room. "Yumi's work is amazing."

Janis slipped a card into her pocket, running her finger along its sharp edge. Outside, the cold air hit her with its mix of car fumes, cigarette smoke and the perfume of a woman in a green vinyl coat who cut across her path.

Janis was putting on her coat to go home when Kayla handed her the black tablecloths.

"I'd return them myself," Kayla said, "but I'm not the one he asked about the other day."

For two long weeks Janis hadn't seen Bjorn. When she

reached his floor, her heart was beating like a huge Japanese drum. Bjorn opened the door looking alarmed.

Stepping back, he put his hands in his pockets. "I was just opening a Merlot to celebrate."

"What's the occasion?" Janis scanned the room. He was alone.

"A manufacturer in New York is interested in my designs. I'm going in a few weeks to meet them."

"Congratulations!"

Bjorn hesitated, then stepped back further. "Why don't you come in?"

Soon they were perched on the stools at his island counter—Bjorn preferred to keep "pigmented beverages" away from his beige leather chair. They discussed the various woods used for furniture, the paintings she'd seen and the possibility of visiting the Art Gallery of Ontario together. The bottle was almost empty when Janis looked at the austere chairs, the prickly red carpet, the platform bed accessible only by ladder—and wondered how anything romantic could begin here.

She pointed at the stereo. "Do you mind if I put something on?"

Bjorn took a small folded towel from the counter and draped it around his neck. "Rachmaninoff, maybe?"

"Can I choose?"

Janis searched without success for a CD that didn't have the yellow Deutsche Grammophon logo. Discouraged, she picked up the disc on the stereo. *Philip Glass: Solo Piano*. On the cover was a man as solemn as Bjorn. She put it on and recognized it as the music from the other time she was there. Impaired by the wine, she couldn't decide if the looping melody was liberating her imagination or putting her into a trance. The combination of the music and odd furniture arrangement reminded her of musical chairs at kids' birthday parties.

Bjorn was sitting on his wood-and-leather armchair. Janis wanted to sit, though not alone. She approached him, about to place her hands on the armrests, about to lean her face toward his. But he cleared his throat and looked away. Only then did she notice that his face was slick with sweat.

"Bjorn! Are you okay?"

"I overheat easily," he said.

"But you're actually dripping. Do you have a fever?" She stepped back.

"It's a condition," he said, blotting himself with the towel.

"My god. Something serious?"

"Hyperhidrosis. Profuse perspiration. It's manageable. With medication. Usually."

"I'm sorry. It must be so uncomfortable."

"Embarrassing, mostly." Bjorn said. "I'll need to increase my dosage before New York. The stress of travel aggravates it. And any excitement."

Despite the dizzying effect of the wine and the frantic, pulsing music, it was suddenly clear to Janis that what this moment demanded, what needed to happen next, was for Bjorn to be rescued from his wretched isolation.

"Don't worry," she said in her gentlest voice. "Perspiration doesn't faze me." She slid the towel from his neck and patted it against the glistening beads on his forehead. He closed his eyes. Encouraged, Janis raised her right foot and inserted it through the gap between chair seat and armrest. Too late she realized that completing the manoeuvre of joining him on his chair was going to be tricky.

"Janis, stop," he said.

Stop now? When she wanted nothing more than to convince him that the sweat, the isolation, the shadowy presence of a ferret-loving Yumi—that none of it should get in their way? Holding the armrests for balance, she began to lift her other foot.

"Please!" Bjorn shouted. "This chair is not designed to support the weight of two people!"

He tried to stand and she gripped him, a fleeting embrace before they both tipped sideways, Bjorn breaking their fall to the carpet with one arm, then landing on top of her. The chair tumbled away. Flattened beneath him, his cheek damp against her chest, her first thought was that at least they were lying down together. Bjorn sprang immediately back up.

"Are you hurt?" he asked.

"Are you?" She tried to sit but was dizzy and flopped back. "What about your chair?"

"I don't know. Damn." He put it upright, began examining it.

"I guess I had too much to drink," she said. A pathetic excuse but one to salvage some dignity. She stared at the ceiling and thought of Gary, how their physical needs had always been so clear to each other. "Anyway, you don't have a couch."

"What do you mean?" he asked.

Janis got up. "I mean something two people can sit on together."

"I'm not interested in upholstery," Bjorn said. He returned to the kitchen and plunked the wineglasses into the sink. "But obviously you're not talking about furniture."

"Right. Maybe I'd better be going." She was already at the colossal door, putting on her coat.

"Wait," he said.

She did, but Bjorn, frowning over whatever he wanted to say, said nothing.

On a warm March evening Janis and Kayla stopped outside the gallery. It was so crowded inside that no art was visible. Yumi, however, was easy to spot. Tall with buzz-cut hair and wearing a white tuxedo shirt and pink polka-dot bow tie, she grinned and gestured as she talked with someone. Janis assumed Bjorn was in there. It'd been a week since her botched seduction and they hadn't bumped into each other. Janis worried that her time in Toronto was dwindling toward an uneventful end.

Two men tapped Yumi on the back and she turned, laughing, to hug both at once.

"Kayla," Janis said, "you said she was really serious."

"I only knew her when she was with Bjorn." Kayla headed inside.

It took them a while to get close to Yumi, but she called out, "Hey, Tree Action Kayla!" when she spotted them.

"Hey, Yumi," Kayla said. "This is Janis. She works with me."

"The more tree people, the better. Welcome!"

"We just arrived," Janis said. "I haven't had a chance to see your work."

Yumi gave Janis's shoulder a friendly squeeze. "The video's playing in another room because it's too nuts out here. Kayla, I'm glad you two came. I might need your help with my next project. I'm diving into environmental issues. I got a grant, so I can even pay."

"Sounds appealing."

"I need solid ecology types. A bit of research, some letter writing." Before she could explain, she was pulled away to meet someone.

Janis turned to Kayla. "I'm going to check out this video."

She crossed the room, weaving between people. Yumi's exuberance had charged the very molecules of the room with energy: people chatted and brushed shoulders, so unlike the Gutenmeyer, with its sombre mood and decomposing food. Janis reached the back to find Bjorn there, a lock of hair stuck to his shiny forehead.

"I'm glad you're here," he said. "We should talk. Let's go somewhere for a drink."

"You can't stay?"

He dabbed a folded handkerchief against his forehead. "I showed up as promised. I saw Yumi—literally, saw her. Anyway, it's too hot."

"I'm not leaving. I just got here," she said.

"Drop by my place tomorrow, then. We can talk about New York."

"New York?"

"Come around six."

Janis nodded, surprised that things with Bjorn might be back on track. After he left, she entered the small room where half a dozen people stood watching the video projected on the wall. A black-and-white scene showed Yumi walking on a deserted road between office towers. A suit jacket lay on the ground behind her. As she walked she removed her dress shirt and pants, revealing that her skin was painted a vibrant spring green, the video's only colour. She kept walking, removing her underwear, her bra. Her entire body was green. She stepped onto a sidewalk and into a band of sunlight, glowing as if phosphorescent. Yumi continued walking toward a building until she was facing its mirrored glass. When she pressed her green skin against it, the scene froze and gradually faded, leaving only the white of the gallery walls. People in the room clapped and started leaving but Janis stayed. She wasn't sure what the video meant but it made her feel happy. That seemed like enough.

Janis stood near the island counter.

"I was thinking," Bjorn continued, "I'd like you to come to New York with me. You might really benefit from seeing what's considered the ultimate urban environment."

She stared at him, bothered on a number of levels but particularly that he didn't just use the word *city*. She had come hoping they would get to know one another better, not talk about her cultural enlightenment.

The phone rang in his office and he jumped to get it, grabbing a towel on the way. Janis walked over to the One Chair. She lowered herself onto it, the upright backrest ordering her spine into a stick-straight posture. She couldn't help overhearing him in the other room: "...a rigorous and contentious show at the Design Exchange...a remarkably comprehensive overview..." His voice had a nasal drawl that intensified when he spoke about design.

Soon she heard the patter of his computer keyboard, the frantic rhythm reminding her of the Philip Glass CD. Janis crossed her arms. What was she waiting for, anyway? For him to transform her like Eliza Doolittle with a trip to New York? She'd just begun to feel connected to Toronto and now he was saying Toronto wasn't good enough. Janis slouched in the chair, a tiny rebellion against its design. As she moved, she felt something scrape against the smooth wood—the rivets on her jeans? She froze. Had she damaged the One Chair? In the other room Bjorn cleared his throat and instinctively she sat up. The rivets scraped again. She winced and stood to have a look. Etched into the seat were two parallel scratches. Horrified, she sat again to cover them.

When Bjorn returned he sank into the plastic chair across from her, rubbing his hands together. Looking at him, she knew with absolute clarity that she didn't want to go to New York. Not now and not with Bjorn.

"It's beautiful outside," she said. "Let's get some fresh air."

Bjorn talked the whole way down in the elevator and didn't stop until they were at the sidewalk. Janis, silently rehearsing how to break the news about his masterpiece, heard nothing. She willed herself to look directly at him. His forehead was damp again and she fought the urge to wipe it with her mitten.

"Something just happened," she said.

"Where?" He glanced around.

"No. In your living room. An accident. I'm so..."

He looked blankly at her.

"My jeans, they kind of—well...scratched your chair. There's a mark. Two marks. I'm really, really sorry."

Eye to eye with her, Bjorn stared as the beads of sweat along his brow bulged and trickled. "Ah, damn," he said in a quiet voice, "that's not good."

"I'll pay for the damage. Whatever is needed." Janis waited for him to erupt.

"Well, the thing is...that's precisely what a prototype is for—a test of real-life conditions. Obviously the polyurethane finish is inadequate. I'll need to try something else." He smiled. "Thank you. It's the bitter reality for any design, but the wear and tear of everyday use has to be factored in. I'll discuss it with the manufacturer when we're in New York."

Janis stared into the eyes that had so enthralled her and wondered if they saw anything outside the head they belonged to.

"Um, something else," she said. "New York. It's a generous offer but I'm probably going to be too busy. I've just picked up some extra work. And I need to go get started on it. Now, in fact."

It was true. True that right then she wanted nothing more than to sink into books about trees. City trees. It was related to Yumi's project, but it was also about things Janis wanted to find out about for herself: like how to make city streets more hospitable to trees, maybe even to hemlocks. She'd discovered a stash of books on the subject at the library. There was also, she'd learned, a university in nearby Guelph that offered a program in landscape architecture, something she might look into.

"You need to work *now*?" Bjorn asked. "I thought we could go for dinner. If you can't join me for the trip, this is my only free evening before I leave."

"Maybe when you get back?" She gave him a goodbye hug and left. When she turned to wave, he was already inside.

Janis walked west on King past buildings candied in the pink light of a spring sunset. The street hummed with people charging home or heading out for a drink or cramming in the day's last errand, all hurrying to be somewhere else. She slowed to have a look at a thin ash tree planted in an opening in the concrete, just making do in difficult conditions. It had been a long winter. Janis checked the time—enough for an hour at the library—and soon she was whipping along the sidewalk as fast as everyone else.

THE BLOOM

—

THE TREES ARE SENTINELS among the tombstones. High above our heads their branches reach toward one another like fingers trying to touch. Though it's well into May, the trees are still not in leaf, and many look half dead, worse this spring than last.

My thoughts return to Joan as I walk with several colleagues under the canopies of branches toward the chapel for her funeral. Outside the modest brick building is a crowd of curious strangers, attracted as much by the rare affliction that changed her life as by her decision on how to deal with it, a decision that baffled everyone. I would be just as puzzled were it not for a chance encounter with Joan a year ago.

The only evidence of the natural world on that April afternoon was a stubborn mound of blackened snow in the parking lot of the shopping plaza and, right above, a low dull cloud going nowhere. Mired in deadlines and late evenings at the office, I was grabbing a week's worth of dinners so Gregory couldn't accuse me of neglecting familial responsibilities. The last person I expected to run into out on her own in public—the last person I remotely wanted to see, in any case—was Joan.

But there she was, walking just ahead, her condition not visible from behind. It was the camel-hair coat I recognized, not the short wavy brown hair she'd stopped bleaching. No surprise that salon visits would be out of the question. Shame washed over me. Since Joan had taken a leave of absence the previous summer, my only contact had been a get-well e-card to which she hadn't replied. Our relationship still bore the strain from a company restructuring two years before—we'd both survived but not before months of relentless scheming to outshine the other. Truthfully, that wasn't the real reason for my distance: it was the terror of seeing Joan's affliction with my own eyes.

I was far from alone on this—we all shuddered at the mention of it. And joked about it too, quietly, guiltily—spluttering over the image of her decorating herself for Christmas. We'd heard about appointments with elite specialists who advised on this recent, but rare, biological phenomenon. We'd wondered why she didn't prune it down, or at least have it surgically removed as someone in California had done. Instead, Joan was apparently opting for a wait-and-see approach along with a reclusive existence at home—shocking for a woman who had once thrived in frenetic twelve-hour days.

Her pace was slow, so unlike the old Joan whose trainer-sculpted legs propelled her across the office carpet like a speedboat on a placid lake. Her gait was also different. Of course there would have to be a change to that—and here she was wearing flat shoes—but this new gentleness to her step intrigued me. This from the woman who had danced at the office party in six-inch stilettos, fists punching the air above our heads.

She stopped and began scooping around in her purse. Several metres behind, heart thumping, I was on the verge of bolting. As if sensing my presence, she turned.

"Clarice!" she half-shouted.

My feet dragged me closer and I managed a facsimile of surprised delight. Meanwhile people passed with either bemused glances or nasty smirks, presuming some kind of prank: a woman, otherwise conventionally dressed, whose winter coat bulged ridiculously at the front just below her left shoulder. The extension of fabric was a close match to the rest of the coat and must have been custom sewn. It looked as though a violin was underneath, poised to be played.

"How are things? How's the family?" I asked, attention fixed on her small, angular face, bare of makeup and yet remarkably luminescent, her eyes both dark and lively.

"Anita's just finished first year at McGill."

"Business, right?"

"Switching to psychology. New interest."

She smiled conclusively, as if that was all the news she had. No mention of her husband, Jonathan, though I was itching to know how he was handling her transformation. He was likely immersed as usual in his law practice.

Joan asked about Gregory and the twins, knowing I hardly had time for them, what with the recent expansion of our division and the extra burden of some of her previous responsibilities. I provided the requisite niceties. Meanwhile, there it was, under her coat, *protruding, protruding, protruding.* Its very proximity nauseated.

A young woman passed by pushing a stroller. Noticing the bulge, she gasped and sped off as though to protect her child. Joan looked sharply away. What she must have had to endure! Scrutiny, ridicule, rudeness and who knew what else? And yet here she was, getting on with her life. How, though, had she gotten to this plaza? Fitting behind a steering wheel would be as inconceivable as a ride on public transit. Maybe she would ask me for a lift home. The urge to flee burbled up again.

"We've missed you at the office," I said, a lie she considered as she squinted at the sky.

Then she looked me straight on. "You have time for a coffee?"

She was already turning eagerly toward JavaWorld. I followed her in and to a table at the back. I stood there clammy with dread as she began to unfasten a series of tiny clasps on the protruding coat panel.

"Let me get the coffee," I blurted.

"Water for me. It's good for—" Her eyes lowered demurely to look at it, even as I kept my eyes trained on hers. "Especially in winter. It prevents desiccation."

Stomach lurching from the thought of it wedded to her flesh, I turned and wove around the tables to the counter. I ordered and paid, spilling coins across the counter, while the cashier stared at my trembling hands like they were the only interesting thing he'd seen that day.

Joan accepted the water and gulped half. I sat, glancing at the other patrons who were oblivious not only to Joan, but to what I was now forced to confront: the tree branch growing out of her.

"So—" I began.

"Listen, Clarice, just don't. There's no need to pussyfoot around, for Christ's sake. Take a good long look. Go ahead: look at it."

The branch, so the story went, had emerged through the skin below her left clavicle the previous summer: a slender horizontal stem like a curious finger reaching out. The third case in North America, but the first ever of *Prunus communis*, a common fruiting cherry. The stem had thickened and lengthened into a proper branch and now sported many twigs. The whole thing was about the size of a child's umbrella. I had always pictured the branch with leaves—the previous autumn an astounded colleague had described sublime oranges and yellows—but on this spring day it was still bare. Dotted along the twigs, however, were coppery green buds that swelled with the promise of blossoms.

"It's...unbelievable," I said.

"Yes, yes—and?"

"And at the same time, it looks almost, well, natural."

Her eyes widened. "I can't tell you how fantastic it is to hear you say that, Clarice. It is natural. And, you know, I feel great."

"You look better than ever," I conceded, sad for the wintery pallor of my own aging skin.

"Uh-huh. It's the photosynthesis. Chlorophyll, right? It's phenomenal."

I nodded, scrambling to recall elementary school science.

"My god, the energy it gives me! And also a kind of mellow happiness. A sunny disposition. Although I admit that hosting this is a bit cumbersome."

Cumbersome! I could only imagine a life upside down. Sleeping under a blanket would be tricky, not to mention sex, and it would barely fit in a shower stall—could it even be cleaned, let alone towel-dried?

"I don't mean to be presumptuous," I said, "but from what I've heard, removal is now an option." It was a running topic at coffee breaks: why not just have the damn thing cut off, use some kind of growth inhibitor cream.

The joy on her face evaporated. She rested her hands on the table, one cupped over the other. "You sound like the doctors, Clarice. Yes, they are concerned about continued growth affecting things. Like my balance. And the root system's a bit unsightly in places. Varicose roots." Her fingers fanned across her abdomen, then she winced. "Sorry. People can't deal with too much detail. I do understand that. But here's the thing: I've never felt better. I'm outside all the time. Drawn like a magnet to the sun and out into the woods behind the house."

"I guess, to be with other trees must be—"

"Listen, Clarice," she said. "That's only part of it. I'm going on gut instinct here. I don't know any better than anyone why this happened to me, someone who's never given a shit about nature. I mean—how many cases in the world? Twenty? And I'm one of them? Why? Maybe I'll never know. But simply cutting it off without understanding feels wrong. And here's the main thing—what nobody seems to give a damn about—it cannot survive without its human host. This much they know: when it's cut off, no matter what is done to salvage the roots, it dies." She glanced at it with a look of maternal fondness. "So on it grows. With my blessing."

"But," I began, struggling for a delicate approach, "have the doctors told you what to expect?"

"Christ, the doctors! The damned specialists! I've seen so many—too many! And none of them help much, except to annoy the hell out of me. They keep tossing out probable outcomes: arthritis, hip fracture, insects, dermatitis."

"Well, those do sound concerning." I was surprised the complications wouldn't be more dire.

"You know what I say to them?" she said.

I shook my head, cowed as I had been on many occasions by the intensity of her stare.

But her eyes softened again and so too did her voice as she touched one of the twigs. "I say to them: imagine delicate white petals unfurling, followed by soft green leaves. Imagine the sun warming this bark. Think of its sweet sap, vital as blood. I say to them: appreciate this miracle, this celebration of natural process in harmony with humanity. *Marvel* at it."

She lifted the water in a silent toast and finished it in one prolonged gulp. Then she looked across the room to the view outside of concrete, filthy cars and that damn low-lying cloud. Her expression suggested she saw an entirely different scene, one that was much, much better. Joan had never been one to proselytize about anything other than the making and spending of money. That she'd wax poetic about flower buds was odder than the branch itself.

Her fingers toyed with one of the twigs. "Todd has been the only one to get me past all the worries and focused on the possibilities."

"Todd?" I asked, trying to catch up to her again.

"Without my body as host, the branch cannot live. I have a responsibility. And Todd has the expertise."

"What sort of doctor is he?"

"I'm done with doctors. Todd is an arbourist."

It took me a moment to absorb that one. "Well, okay. I can see how he could offer a valuable perspective on your condition. But, forgive me, it's just that—what about *your* health?"

"I'm Todd's patient now. And of course, *patient*'s not even the right word. Let's face it—I fascinate him. Actually, I fascinate us both." She tucked a curl of hair behind her ear.

"Does he have any answers, though? I mean, about how things will go—for you?"

Really, though, I wanted to know more about what her husband, Jonathan, thought about all this. And her daughter, who'd switched to psychology, probably because of this sea change in her mother's psyche.

"Something very special might happen. If I allow it."

Before she could explain, her phone rang. As she spoke, she stared toward the window again, and I examined the sturdy, reddish brown bark that in places gleamed with a silvery patina. The branch, I realized, did not alarm me quite as much as it had only minutes earlier.

"That was Todd," she said after the call. "He'll be by in a minute to pick me up." Joan must have guessed my thought. "He has a van, Clarice. With enough room for me in the back. You might as well know: Jonathan and I are taking a breather."

"I'm so sorry."

"Don't be. Things had run their course." The old Joan I knew fixed me with a dark look. Then she shrugged like we were discussing a house cleaner who hadn't worked out. "It's all for the better. Why put him through more grief?"

We got up and I helped her into her coat, though she insisted on leaving it open, the branch jutting out for all to see. She was magnificent. Not just because of the promise of blossoms along the twigs growing out of her. But because she exuded an extraordinary energy. Whatever the reasons or the explanation for the branch itself, it was truly miraculous. I was happy for her.

We emerged from the coffee shop to find the day as changed as my feelings. Sunlight leaked through the low cloud and car windshields rebroadcast the brightness in all directions. Even bits of plastic debris embedded in the crusty snow mountain sparkled like jewels. Most impressive of all, the sunlight illuminated the creamy white flower buds, and the copper branches echoed the brown of Joan's eyes.

"What a day!" she said.

"We should get together soon with the gang from work," I suggested, though I sensed this would be our last meeting.

"Of course," she said, squinting toward the parking entrance, not even pretending to care about regular things anymore. She didn't need my pity or concern. The conversation in the coffee shop had served its purpose of providing the info I would pass on to the others, along with proof that she was as much in control of her life as she had ever been, though now with profound joy. She had likely already made her decision by then.

We said our goodbyes and I began to walk away. I was compelled to look back, though. Joan stood waiting where I'd left her. In that brief moment a small shape swooped down from the building canopy. A bird! It fluttered lower, having spotted the branch—the only one in sight—but then noticed the human head. The bird hovered, as though deliberating, while Joan, unaware, raised her arm to wave at an approaching green van. The bird rose swiftly and flew away.

In the weeks following our encounter, the branch would have bloomed. Flowers, then leaves and, ultimately, cherries. Maybe Joan and Todd ate a few together. It must have been strange at first, but then, after a nervous laugh or two, perhaps they each took a tentative bite, marvelling at the succulence of the red fruit, the product of her body's remarkable fusion with nature. Through the summer, the branch would have flourished as the twigs continued growing and the leaves matured and darkened through several shades of green. Inside her, too, growth would continue: the fine tendril-like roots reaching more deeply into her body. I imagined Joan and Todd's relationship deepening as well, bonded by a love for the branch. By autumn, I heard she was living on Todd's acreage north of the city. I pictured them spending a peaceful winter together, keeping her as comfortable as possible until spring, when the ground would thaw.

Todd, a craggy-faced old man whose advanced age surprises us all, gives the eulogy. He speaks of Joan's dedication to the branch: how she valued it as a living organism in its own right, how she honoured its needs before her own, how she fully committed herself to ensuring that the branch fulfill its destiny. Since her death, nobody has seen it. According to Todd, it is no longer a branch at all but a sapling, a sapling that is thriving on his forested property.

I picture it planted alone in the middle of a clearing with space and sunlight to grow but protected from the wind by the surrounding trees that themselves struggle to survive. Under the soil, the sapling's roots are still fused to Joan's remains. Above ground, its twigs swell with buds, promising the first glimpse of pure white petal, readying to bloom.

THE BLUE DRESS

———

"SO, HERE IT IS." Jeffrey's arm took in the low buildings and beach and calm South China Sea, as if that was all Clay needed to know about Stanley Village. He pointed to exclusive town-houses along the crest of a mountain. "And up there, where Nance and I will live. One day."

"Lucky you," Clay said. "Both of you."

Nance let her hand drop from Jeffrey's and looked at the water. They'd brought Clay to this quieter, scenic side of Hong Kong Island to buy souvenirs. The air here was clean but still humid, the sky white with heat.

"Let's start with a bite," Jeffrey said. "And a drink."

"Chinese or Western?" Nance asked Clay.

"A good ole English pub, Clayton," Jeffrey said in a silly London accent. Parodying the Brits offset the stress of work-ing at a British-owned investment firm. Nance, employed at a small language school run by a Chinese woman who'd learned

English in Birmingham, was just as immersed but weary of this game.

Clay Chau had never been to Asia. A second-generation Canadian, he didn't understand much Chinese, and smiled apologetically at shopkeepers and waiters who mistook him for a local. He accepted whatever he encountered with a pleasant shrug. Nance had only met him once in Toronto and wondered if he had always been this way or was, like herself, more freshly defeated. Clay's girlfriend had recently left him—apparently the reason for this trip.

Jeffrey excused himself to find a bank machine and she and Clay continued along the sidewalk stretching the length of beach. A smattering of people in bathing suits lay on towels. Others in street clothes stepped toward the water, carrying their shoes. A girl in a candy-pink bathing suit turned slowly around, dragging a stick through the sand. Serious and focused, she kept turning until the circle she drew was complete. The first sight of any beach coaxed out Nance's memories of childhood summers at the lake, but this sea was pungent and vast.

She glanced at Clay, who was also looking at the water.

"Jeffrey says you're thinking of a new job."

His eyebrows rose as if his own news surprised him. Clay was an illustrator who'd worked at the same ad agency for years. "Thinking, yes. I'm ready for a change."

"It's good to get away, get some perspective." She said it automatically, then realized how little it applied to her own situation. She'd only followed Jeffrey here, lured by his confidence.

"I'm really enjoying Hong Kong," he said. "It's great."

"It's a strange place, though," she ventured, hoping he would say something unexpected, something that really mattered to him. Then she'd be free to say more too. But what could she really expect him to understand of her knotted feelings? She was the stranger here. While she couldn't warm up to the other expatriates, Jeffrey's social immersion had been seamless, like his joining the American running group that ran dozens-strong through the streets. He'd also embraced the expatriate drinking culture, that and the unrelenting nightlife she usually opted out of. Give Hong Kong a year, she'd told herself. And now she had.

"Jeffrey seems to love it here," Clay offered.

"He loves the culture," she said, watching a Chinese family—parents, kids, grandparents—unpack a picnic lunch beside the beach parking lot. "The money culture, at least. Making it and spending it."

Clay brightened. "He's good at making money. Really good."

Nance hesitated. He might not want to be a party to her griping. She watched several fishing boats returning to the harbour. "There are things I like here. Living by the sea. The mild winter. Still, I prefer Toronto. Jeffrey won't leave, though."

Jeffrey fell in love with her during the last months of her father's long illness. Nance had navigated doctors and treatments, and when she could manage a break, Jeffrey, with his white-blond hair and good looks, had been easy to reach for. He'd organized the parts of her life she had no energy to deal with: car repairs, refunds on courses she hadn't completed. His bed was the one place she could escape illness and hospitals. Five months into their relationship, her father died. Numb for weeks, she stayed away. But when she returned to Jeffrey, it was to news of his transfer to Hong Kong.

Clay was frowning, about to say something Nance wanted to hear. But Jeffrey caught up to them. He held an open bag of shrimp-flavoured chips. Knowing she hated the smell, he tipped the bag toward Clay.

"Aren't we about to eat?" she asked.

He patted his wallet. "We certainly are, my dear. And lunch is on me."

Was this just for Clay's amusement? He knew she was sensitive about how little she earned compared to him. It bothered Nance not to have more money of her own in case things went wrong between them.

After lunch they returned to the hot street leading to the crowded souvenir market, a narrow lane with white tarps draped overhead. Open storefronts were packed with clothing, embroidered purses, jade bracelets and T-shirts with Chinese characters extolling noble ideas like harmony and strength. Nance led Clay from shop to shop. He had a sister, several nephews and his mother to buy for. Six days into his visit, he hadn't purchased anything. Jeffrey barely glanced at the merchandise as he strolled. He did manage to interest himself in some tiny figurines of Chinese couples from ancient times in various sexual positions, and held one up to make a show of studying it. He lifted his eyes to Nance, a reminder of the night before. She smiled, but the moment sank away in the stifling market air, and Jeffrey wandered ahead.

Nance approached a rack of colourful silk clothing. "Maybe your sister would like these, Clay."

He nodded but seemed overwhelmed by the selection.

A blue dress caught her eye. She rarely bought dresses, but this one was different: a modern style with a mandarin collar, the blue a deep shade she was drawn to. The price was less than expected and could likely be reduced with haggling.

"I don't know what size she is," Clay muttered.

"Those silk purses are a safer bet, then," she said, pointing to a nearby table.

He wandered away and she turned again to the dress.

A small cubicle in one corner of the store served as the

change room. Its thin curtain wouldn't quite close. She peeled off her shorts and T-shirt. As she moved, the curtain shifted and reflected in the mirror was the back of Clay's head, the sharp edge of his dark hair touching the pale skin of his neck. She pulled the curtain tighter to the wall and noticed the whiteness of her own skin above the line of her bra. She stepped into the dress, zipped up the side, the soft fabric pressing against her thighs and hips and breasts. It was a bit tight, but the blue matched her eyes.

She slid the curtain aside but didn't step out. "Clay?"

He came up to her and didn't seem to realize where she'd been until his eyes moved over the dress.

"It's synthetic," she said, "but you wouldn't know."

He surprised her then. He reached one hand out and slowly brushed his fingers across the fabric at her waist.

"It's really nice," he said. "You should get it."

She held still even after his hand dropped away.

Jeffrey stood behind the couch, clicking through channels, then gave up and turned off the TV. Clay was napping in the den, their makeshift guest room with a borrowed futon on the floor beside Jeffrey's desk. A week into the trip, he was still jet-lagged.

In the kitchen Nance surveyed the contents of the fridge, deciding they could get by another day without braving the evening crowds at the grocery store. Tomorrow they'd be back to work after the weekend with Clay. She peered out to the living room where Jeffrey flipped through a business magazine.

"He's going to be up all night if he sleeps too long," she said.

"I'll take him out after dinner. Tire him out again." Jeffrey came into the kitchen. "That promotion's coming soon," he said. "We'll move to Causeway Bay, closer to my office and other Westerners. You'll meet more people. You can quit work if you want."

But she liked her job teaching everyday conversation to hopeful emigrants. She liked the shy exchanges with her middle-aged students, their curiosity about Canadian life, how they prompted her to learn Cantonese. She liked their shocked laughter when she bungled the tricky tones, the meanings of the words changed in ways they were too embarrassed to explain.

Jeffrey let go her hand and stretched his arms. "Work is going to be nuts this week. The report's due and Murray's still off sick. I'll be late most nights." He squeezed the back of his neck but his eyes widened like he was pleased.

"What about Clay?" she asked.

"The timing's lousy, I know. All he did last week was wander around alone. You can show him around, can't you?"

"Tomorrow I could. I get off early."

"You deserve some fun. I've been a colossal drag lately." He leaned close and pressed his cheek against her hair. "You could come with me to that cocktail reception on Tuesday. Show off that new dress."

Clay emerged, bleary-eyed, from the den in a crumpled T-shirt and shorts. "How long did I sleep?"

"It's 2020," Jeffrey said. "Sorry to report that you're forty-something years old, Clayton. So much you missed!"

Clay stood just outside the tiny kitchen, smiling. Nance got out the pasta sauce, feeling his gaze on her, a reminder of his touch.

Clay phoned her at work in the afternoon, sounding harried. Jackhammers clattered in the background. The city's commotion and heat was getting to him.

"Let's meet at Hong Kong Park," she said. She pictured his eyes, as brown and clear as Chinese tea. "It's calm there. And the air's better."

Diesel fumes mingled with the fragrance of garlic and meat as she navigated the crowded sidewalk. She headed for the steep road at the base of the mountain, encouraged by the sight of trees ahead. Jeffrey might be up in his mirrored tower nearby or across the harbour in a meeting. It amazed her how separate their lives were during the blackout hours of work.

Clay sat on the steps at the entrance. He spotted her and waved. The park was large and partly forested and featured a net-covered aviary at one end. They followed the main path past an artificial pond and tidy gardens until they found a narrower path leading up a hill through a naturalized area. Here the air felt drier and fresh. The greenery and the faint scent of soil made the looming skyscrapers seem unimportant and surreal. Clay and Nance kept walking up in comfortable silence, passing an unusual tree, its branches gnarled and expressive. She imagined them stopping at the tree and standing so close to it and to each other that everything else would fade away.

"Have you spent the day being mistaken for a local again?" she asked when they reached a flat stretch.

He laughed. "I'm getting used to it. I learned a few words from my grandparents. I wish I knew more."

"Do you feel any connection to Hong Kong?"

"My family came from Guangzhou, so not really. But this is the first place I've been where I'm not in the visible minority. It's a cool feeling."

Just the opposite, this was Nance's first experience as a minority. Though foreigners were common, she was often stared at and wondered if the interest was in a Western woman— whatever that meant to the person staring—or in her specifically. She hadn't thought about it before, the power of anonymity. She had no history here, no connections, was free in some way she hadn't explored.

"I like this park," Clay said. "Thanks for bringing me."

"It's nice to tour with a fellow Canadian. It takes the edge off my homesickness."

"What do you miss most?"

"The spaciousness, I guess. Quiet streets."

"What about family?" he asked.

"With my dad gone, there's really only my cousin and aunt in Halifax. So I'm kind of alone wherever I am."

He considered this, his expression serious. Then he held up his camera. "Let me take your picture."

He had her stand at a spot with a view of the financial district, then brought the camera over to show her. She filled a third of the photo but was still dwarfed by the buildings. In it she looked pleased, if a little bewildered, as if wondering why she was there. A bird called loudly from nearby, drawing her attention to the path leading to the aviary.

"Do you want to see the birds, Clay? Or would you rather eat?"

"Yes to both. A domesticated bird, stir-fried."

She laughed. "There's a restaurant nearby with a few of those."

After dinner, they climbed the stairs of a covered footbridge that spanned a busy road. Nance liked being above the traffic and jostling crowds. Up here the only commotion was the argument of signs jutting out from the buildings.

"Should we call Jeff?" Clay asked. "Maybe he's finished work."

Nance stopped at the railing. As the daylight faded, a neon glow was gradually taking over the street. She pictured Jeffrey out with colleagues, sitting too close to someone. "He rarely comes straight home. He likes to unwind with the office gang. Drink, meet new people." She glanced at Clay who peered down at a passing tram. "Things aren't great between us."

"Really? I hadn't realized." Clay frowned.

"He thinks things will be fine if I would just join the gang at the pub. Or go sailing on the weekends. Maybe we're just too different." Clay said nothing. "It's nice to finally get to know you. And it's good for Jeffrey and me, having someone else around. It's a good distraction for you too, I guess," she added. "Jeffrey told me about your breakup. How you needed to get away from Toronto."

"I'd always wanted to come here. The timing was right."

The cars kept rushing by below them. All that urgent momentum made standing still feel odd.

"You were together a long time, right?" she asked but he didn't answer.

A group of Chinese men in suits walked by, talking loudly. She checked her watch. "It's Happy Hour. We could go for a drink."

He looked straight at her for a moment. But he wasn't smiling and Nance was uncertain about what she wanted, except to be in some way more lost tonight than she already was. She studied the crowds below, the workday's frenetic pace gradually turning languid. She could pull Clay into the night with her, away from everyone, down to the quiet harbour where the still black water would keep any secret. Would he join her in a mistake like that?

"Maybe we should get back," he said. "Jeff might be home."

Jeffrey's name lingered in the cool air. She rubbed her bare arms. "I guess you're pretty tired," she said. "You've walked everywhere today."

"Let's take a cab, okay?" He pushed away from the railing. "You must be tired too."

The apartment was dark when Nance opened the door. She flicked on the light, dropped her purse on a chair.

"Jeff mentioned all of us going out for dinner tomorrow night," Clay said.

"That's right. After a client thing he and I have to attend."

Clay pointed toward the den, where his clothes lay heaped on his suitcase. "I'll have to buy something better to wear."

"Knowing what a great shopper you are, you'd better start first thing in the morning."

"Ha. True." He paused, camera still slung over his shoulder. The quiet of the room seemed to underline Jeffrey's absence. She said goodnight and they headed to their rooms.

Nance fell slowly asleep and into a dream. She was walking down an empty Hong Kong sidewalk at night past closed and shuttered shops. Clay walked with her. Music played nearby, a familiar Chinese song. She was about to ask if he recognized it, but he stopped and without warning slid his hands around her waist. His lips touched her neck and though her gut sank with fear, she wanted this and was about to respond. But then he was pulling at her shirt with an urgency that didn't make sense. She woke to Jeffrey against her in the dark, his leg slung over hers, hand sliding over her breasts. She wanted to slip back to the dream even as her body warmed to their familiar pattern: her hands finding his shoulders, his fingers tugging at her pyjamas. But he was moving too fast, pressing too hard, smelling of booze.

When he lowered his face for a kiss she turned her head away.

"Jesus, Nance." He rolled off her.

"Sorry."

"Sorry, sorry," he grumbled, but his breathing began to slow as he gave in to sleep.

She got up. Shutting the door behind her, she stood in the dark living room. The den light was on, the door partly open.

"Clay?" she whispered.

"You're up?" he said, opening the door from where he sat on the futon.

"Can't sleep," she said.

He held up a book, something about business in China. "Here, this should do the trick."

She sat on the floor just outside the doorway. "Jeffrey's drunk."

"I know. We talked. His job's pretty intense."

"It's what he wanted," she said, staring up at Jeffrey's desk, papers in neat piles, labelled and prioritized. "He always knows what he wants. And then he gets it."

"That's a good thing, isn't it?" Clay said, his voice suddenly sharp. He ran his finger along the edge of the book.

"Is something wrong?" she asked.

"I've been accused of the opposite: not knowing what I want."

"Accused?"

"One of the many things Tanya said. Like it was partly my fault, her cheating. I heard a lot of shit like that. He worked in my office too."

"That must have been awful."

"That's one way to put it."

"Well, I'm glad you were able to get away for this holiday, in any case. You've been so good to talk with."

"I've spent the last few months pretty convinced I'm no good to anyone for anything." He exhaled slowly and put the book down.

"Before Jeffrey came home, I was having a dream. A nice one. It was quiet and there was even this beautiful Chinese music."

"I wish I had dreams like that. Not everyone chasing me with swords."

"I'm serious," she said, but smiled. "It's the first dream I've had that takes place here. In Hong Kong."

"Nice. Maybe it means you like Hong Kong more than you realize."

"I'm a mess, though," she said. "I feel like one."

"Look. You're practically alone, and you're not exactly falling apart. You like your job. And today, showing me around, you were really happy."

"Because you inspired me."

"C'mon," he said. "I inspire no one." Then he looked at her. "You're okay, Nance. That's what I think."

He leaned back as if something had been settled. From the street far below came the droning of cars, mellower than daytime. Otherwise it was quiet. No crickets like back home, but the night here had its own kind of peace.

When she returned to bed, Jeffrey shifted in his sleep to lie against her.

"Where'd you go?" he murmured, and she closed her eyes to think through what Clay had said about her being okay.

Nance wore the blue dress and met Jeffrey at the lounge of the Furama Hotel, his pale hair easy to spot in the crowd. He kissed her cheek and led her into the eddy of mingling guests as servers navigated the room with silver trays of canapés and drinks. Jeffrey handed Nance a martini and introduced her to his client. When the conversation turned to business, she excused herself to wander through the room past white leather sofas and towering potted palms. She glanced back at Jeffrey, now talking to a slim Chinese woman in an elegant silver dress. He kept leaning toward her face as though sharing a confidence, his hand at her elbow. He wore his good suit. Jeffrey always looked pleased in a suit, like he'd achieved an elevated state of being. He was handsome and in his element. She was happy for him.

Afterwards, in the taxi, Jeffrey told the driver to take them to Aberdeen Harbour.

"What's up?" she asked. She'd expected they would meet Clay in nearby Causeway Bay.

"I had a brainwave. Dinner on Lamma Island. Juliana Wu gave me a tip on where to hire a private yacht."

"Is that the woman you were talking to?"

"She's whip-smart. She'll be running our client's Asia division before long. She works her gorgeous ass off."

"But still finds time to take her gorgeous ass on a boat trip," Nance said, "just to get a plate of steamed fish."

"What is that supposed to mean?"

It had only been a joke. What did Nance really care about another woman in Jeffrey's orbit? She shook her head. "Anyway, isn't Lamma really casual? We're so dressed up."

He brushed something off his pants. "We're in costume. Think of it that way."

She didn't like his harsh tone. Something was eating him. Maybe she was a letdown after his sophisticated colleagues.

"I *have* been thinking of it that way, actually," she said.

She looked out as the taxi sped up a steep overpass just metres from dingy concrete apartments. She longed to get away from the filth and the crowding and all the rushing around.

"That the dress Clay picked out for you?" he asked, looking out the window.

"It's the dress I picked out for myself."

"I like it."

"So do I."

"It's blue, like you."

She let the comment pass. "We're still meeting Clay, aren't we?"

"Looking forward to seeing him?" She turned to meet his sharp eyes studying her. "Me too," he said. "It'll be fun. He needs an evening with his good friend and his good friend's girlfriend. And he needs to get over Tanya, stop being Mr. Sensitive about everything."

"As if there's something wrong with being sensitive," she snapped.

"I know all about it, Nance. Lots of things I know about Clay—what he hears and what he says. He's my buddy, remember? I know more about him than you'd ever care to." He jabbed the button to lower the window and warm air flooded in. "Smell the sea?" he said, looking out as glimpses of water flashed between the buildings they raced by. "That's the smell of our dinner."

On the yacht, Jeffrey joked with Clay, as if their short journey under a pink evening sky was just one more good segment in a perfect day. Nance sat away from them, watching the approach to the small island. The land rose steeply into low mountains. The only sign of life was a row of modest one-storey restaurants along a raised pier. She was grateful now that Jeffrey had sprung this on them, a special experience for Clay, who laughed when told how overdressed they all would be. On first seeing her in the blue dress, Clay had offered a pleasant but obscure smile. It reminded her of that morning's first waking thought: Clay's touch in the store could not be bettered.

They docked at the end of the harbour alongside smaller boats. Jeffrey offered his hand to help her onto the pier, given the tightness of her dress. Their destination was the last of the restaurants at the far end, a concrete building open to the pavement with metal tables and chairs scattered both inside and out. Large tanks of fish and shellfish lined the inside wall. One tank was crammed with mottled grey fish. Swerving between them was an eel, its slick dark body circling the tank. Nance put revulsion aside to bring her face close and watched its fierce black eyes scan the mirrored glass, looking for the way out.

The restaurant was half full. They settled at one of the tables inside, chair legs scraping the tile floor. Jeffrey looked around and grinned. Everyone else was Chinese, proof of the place's authenticity. Clay kept glancing at her, as if sensing tension between her and Jeffrey, though the boat ride had all but erased it. His attention felt cloying when she just wanted to breathe and relax.

The waiter brought glasses and large bottles of local San Miguel beer, and Jeffrey toasted Clay. "Here's to better times ahead. She didn't deserve you, bud." He looked at Nance before taking a long drink of beer.

Clay hesitated, then drank with him.

Jeffrey slapped his glass down on the metal table. "Which is why I support your idea, Clayton. It's a big change but the timing couldn't be better."

"Well, it still depends on my uncle. I have to talk more with him when I get back home."

"What idea are we talking about?" Nance asked.

"Just a business opportunity my uncle proposed," Clay said, tapping his fingers against his glass. "He has an importing company in Shenzhen. He might want me to help run it. If I like it here."

"Shenzhen's close enough to the border that he could live here in Hong Kong and commute," Jeffrey explained. "The dragon is rising! Here's to China and capitalism! And Clay's repatriation!" Other diners looked over with interest.

"It's all just talk at this point," Clay said to Nance. "It came up today at lunch."

"You had lunch together?"

"In Central. Then Jeff helped pick out my shirt and tie."

"Which is why you look so fucking sharp, right?" Jeffrey said, and laughed.

As the beer flowed, Clay spoke more freely about his plans, and Nance began to revisit the past few days. Why had she allowed herself to believe she and Clay shared a special connection, that he might miraculously lift her from her fog? Jeffrey, luxuriating in his money-focused world, seemed just as remote.

"It's going to be a blast setting you up here, Clay," Jeffrey said, and drained the rest of his beer. "First priority is finding you a place to stay when you come back. I can't have another man loose in our apartment, can I?"

Nance pushed her chair back and got up.

"Joking, Nance. Just a joke. Come on." He reached for her hand.

"A crappy joke, Jeff," Clay said with a weak laugh.

"I just need some air," she said.

Jeffrey stood and came around the table until he was breathing into her hair. "Sorry, Nance," he whispered. "I'm a bit hammered, that's all. I'm an ass sometimes. But you know I love you."

"It's okay," she said, and touched his arm. His sleeves were rolled up to the elbow, his skin tanned. "I just need a minute alone."

She walked out toward where the boats were moored, the

clatter from the restaurants fading. She passed the yacht they'd hired for the night and several empty fishing boats. People lived in a village on the other side of this island. Expatriates too, she'd once heard. People who didn't mind the commute to Hong Kong and preferred the quiet, natural setting. She could imagine living here.

She glanced back to see the lights along the restaurant roofs had turned on, reflected on the water's surface like strings of pearls. The blue of the water was deepening, darker now than her dress. At the end of the pier ahead of her, several ram-shackle boats were anchored. In one, an old Chinese couple sat together, hunched over a meal of noodles. The man noticed her. It must have surprised him to see this Western woman standing there alone and so dressed up.

"You want boat home?"

She nodded but then answered in Cantonese: "*Hoy* Hong Kong Island?"

His wife waved her closer.

"*Gay do cheen?*" Nance asked. She had some cash, not much. When she got to the other side, she'd call Jeffrey's cell to let him know she was fine. Then she'd decide where to go.

"Very clever!" The man rose, still holding his bowl. "One hundred fifty Hong Kong dollar."

"*Ho-lah,*" she said.

The noodles were put aside and he helped her into the boat, pointing to a bench near the front.

The sky and water were merging into the darkest blue. But the water was the more intriguing, its surface rippling like silk. The dread she'd known through her father's illness seemed to lie just below, his fear of dying and then her own, of doing nothing with her life. She'd thought coming with Jeffrey to Hong Kong was brave, but really it was just a different way of feeling safe, under his protection. As the boat moved farther out, the water became black. How easy it would be to lean over the edge and give it her hand, let it take her.

The old man called out something above the noise of the motor, and she looked back to where he sat steering, dim in the lamplight, his wife quiet beside him.

"Where you from?" the old man shouted.

Before she could answer, his wife pointed. They were emerging from the harbour and into view of Hong Kong Island. Even this residential side of the island, with its densely packed condo towers and luxury townhouses, lit the night like a carnival. Sitting in the boat with this old couple, so removed from all of that, so sublimely modest, Nance pictured a different life here. Somewhere quiet, on her own. She would find a way to tell Jeffrey, first about leaving him, and then about staying.

FALLOUT

We were alone in a basement parking garage, surrounded by bare concrete walls and the smell of gasoline. The building superintendent had shown us down two hours earlier. He glanced at our photo IDs but didn't ask questions, as if the government always sent university students to his door with strange work to carry out. We were supposed to confirm the square footage of all the underground areas. Later we would use Emergency Planning Department formulas to figure out the capacity of the garage. Not for cars, but for people. How many people could fit in there if the Cold War turned hot?

I was paired with Craig to cover Scarborough because that's where we lived, each of us back home for the summer. In September, Craig would start his second year of engineering in Kingston. I would be downtown studying photography and only had the job because of my uncle Les in Ottawa. I held the clipboard with a copy of the floor plan and Craig carried the measuring tape. Week after week we confirmed wall lengths together, basement after basement.

At our training seminar, they had shown us an old black and white film. In it a man brushed fallout from his shoulders like it was nothing more than dandruff. Sirens shrieked while he and his neighbours filed calmly down the basement stairs. They sat playing cards underground, as if that's all it would take to wait out the half-life of radioactivity outside. I glanced past Craig to the exit, remembering the hyped-up TV movie the night before about the Bomb destroying a small American city. Streets choked with stalled cars and people running everywhere and nowhere until the wave of heat rolled right through them. In a flash they were skeletons. Then dust. I had gone to bed in a sickened daze and woke later. I must have screamed because when my eyes adjusted to the dark, and the details of my room emerged, there in the doorway stood my mom, just like when I was younger. But she didn't say anything this time. All I wanted to hear was that everything would be okay, but what could anyone say to erase a fear of the bomb?

I held the end of the tape against the corner of the wall. "This place is huge," I called out to Craig. "We won't finish here today." We still had three other apartment buildings in the complex to verify. At the City archives the day before, we'd copied their garage and basement layouts from old blueprints.

At the other end of the wall, Craig leaned in close to read the number on the tape. He denied that he needed glasses. This small vulnerability appealed to me. He didn't reveal too much of himself, just his interests in things like baseball and heavy metal and the bar where he hung out with his buddies and his girlfriend, things I didn't care about. He wore a blue shirt and beige slacks. The job had a dress code, since no one would open their door to twenty-year-olds in jeans. My own attempt at respectability was a white blouse and navy skirt that restrained my movements. On weekends I dressed only in black and went downtown to see a local band that played the clubs. I liked the singer. Anton shouted bleak lyrics with half-closed eyes and sometimes between sets he would talk to me. I liked that his brown hair looked soft—he hadn't dyed or spiked it like the others. On the back of his leather jacket he had painted an "A" inside a circle. Like me, he was interested in a government-free society based on peaceful cooperation, everyone on equal footing. The others talked about Molotov cocktails and running wild through the streets. Anton was more thoughtful. Gentle too, I hoped, despite the people he hung out with.

"Twenty metres, sixty-three centimetres," Craig called, his voice hollowed out by all that empty space. No one was around. Sometimes people came in to get their cars, but they would never guess what we were up to. I recorded the measurement and moved to the next wall.

"Last one before lunch," he said. "Seventeen metres." He walked toward me as I wrote it down. "Let's eat."

I put the clipboard into my knapsack and saw my camera, my change of clothes for later.

"Did you watch the movie last night?" I asked, and when he didn't say anything I looked at him. He was slowly winding the tape back up like he hadn't heard me. "When they drop the bomb," I said, "I hope I'm in my own basement. I want a shelter with booze and a TV."

"Yeah? I wonder what would be on."

I pictured the buzzing test pattern screen, the eeriness of not knowing what was happening. Then I remembered a detail from the movie: the first thing to go was the power. "Sitcoms," I said. "To give us all a few last laughs."

"What if you're unlucky, though," he said, and picked up

his bag. "You'll be outside somewhere and end up in parking level 2B.'"

"Seriously," I said, "no one would actually use these places. It would be complete chaos. It wouldn't be safe above ground for years. Maybe never. This job is a joke."

"It pays well, so who gives a shit?" Craig's voice, hard like the walls around us, surprised me. We had argued before but he didn't usually get this uptight.

He started walking toward the fire exit.

"I guess I do," I said. "I guess it bugs me to be here helping prep for a nuclear war instead of doing something to prevent it."

Craig turned. "But you are here, right? If you hate it that much, why don't you quit?" He stood there halfway to the exit and even in the gloom, his whole body in shadow, I could see how tense he was.

"Whatever," I said, because he was right. I swung my knapsack over one shoulder and followed him out into the bright afternoon.

We ate our sandwiches in silence, sitting on the parched grass of a small hill dotted with pine trees that faced the parking lot. The few cars still around on a workday shimmered like UFOs in the sun's glare. Off by itself was the Pinto that Craig picked me up in each day. It was his mom's and it was clean and smelled of fake lemons and plastic. Hardly anyone was around. It was just massive brick apartments ganged up around asphalt and bland lawns. It felt like everyone had already been evacuated.

Usually on Fridays Craig asked me about my plans for the weekend. I think he expected me to be entertaining because he considered me a bit of a freak, not remotely like the girlfriend he spent weekends with trolling the mall or seeing whatever movie was popular.

"What are you and Kelly up to tonight?" I finally asked.

"No Kelly tonight. I'm partying with friends. What about you?"

I was meeting Anton at a park downtown to take photos of him for the cover of his demo tape. At the bar, between sets, I asked him what effect he wanted for the photos, anything to keep him nearby, his dark ideas, his sweet scoffing smile. I was hoping to leave early, take the bus to the subway. If I was late, Anton wouldn't be the type to hang around, if he even showed up at all.

"I'm going to check out a few record stores," I told Craig. "Nothing special."

"I thought punks partied hardy," he said. "You disappoint me."

This was territory already covered during weeks of lunch hours, but I was glad he seemed his normal self again. "I'm not a punk, remember? I'm a madly scheming anarchist."

"Oh, right. An anarchist who works for the government." He stretched his legs out.

"I'm infiltrating. It's part of the Plan."

"You haven't worn that skirt before," he said, mouth full of sandwich.

I glanced down and tugged the hem to cover more leg. "So?"

"So, it looks good on you."

I could have groaned. I didn't want any kind of weirdness between us. The work was weird enough.

"Piss off," I said, biting into dry bread crust.

"Take it easy, take it easy." He picked at the grass. His slender fingers looked like they'd be good at making things. Maybe he had some corny hobby, like model airplanes.

Craig finished his sandwich, squeezed the plastic wrap into a ball and tossed it up into a nearby pine tree.

"You pig. Some bird will choke on that." But I didn't even try to go get it. We stared into the spiny branches as if the tree belonged to a different world.

Craig stood up and walked down to the car. I looked at his beige slacks, studied his ass as if now I had a right to since he was checking out my legs. He opened the trunk and rummaged around. When he walked back up the hill he was holding a mickey.

"You've got to be kidding," I said.

He sat down again beside me and rubbed his fingers along the label on the bottle, trying to smooth out a corner that was ripped. "Kelly and I broke up," he said.

"That sucks. I'm sorry."

"Two and a half years together. Anyway, screw that." I saw now how tired he was, his eyes a bit red. He glared at the apartment towers. Then he gulped from the bottle and handed it over. It was three-quarters full.

"We won't feel like working," I said. But I drank.

The gin burned down my throat and I thought about how great it would be to drive a really long time, get away from people and buildings to where something nice started. Fields, forests. "Maybe regular things don't matter anymore," I said, "if we're doomed." I brushed my fingers across the tips of the grass.

"Then we don't have to work if we don't want to." He gulped some more. "No one will know."

It was true we'd gotten a lot done the past two weeks, way ahead of schedule. Besides, our supervisor was a moron. "I don't feel like going down there again either," I said.

He was gently sloshing the gin around in the bottle. "We should, though."

But he got up and pulled the car key from his pocket. I got up too and brushed off my skirt.

"I was thinking of leaving early anyway," I said, "to go downtown."

Anton had smiled when I agreed to take pictures of him. But then his gaze had slipped past my shoulder to the others in the bar, and at the end of the night he left with a woman with pierced lips and nose. I'd adopted a mild version of the crowd's angry look, but my eyes leaked the truth: what I wanted was warmth.

The drone of an engine in the sky made us look up. We kept looking up until from behind one of the apartments an airplane appeared and inched across the turquoise sky. I often thought about the way it all might happen. I hoped I'd be in bed asleep and wouldn't see it coming. I wouldn't see the flash, brighter than the sun, brighter than anything anyone has ever seen. I wouldn't see the cloud, white and soft, spreading with cruel grace in every direction, turning everything—apartment buildings and cars and sparrows and pine trees and people caught mid-sentence, people arguing or falling in love—into the same meaningless grey dust. The cloud, like a blanket, would simply smother me before I could wake.

We walked down the hill to the Pinto and got in. Craig revved the engine like it was some hot vehicle and it cracked us up for a minute.

"Where you headed, miss?" he asked.

"The subway. But I don't need to be there for another three hours." I stared out the window to hide my smile.

"Well then, I'll drive very, very slow."

I laughed, and kept staring out.

He drove us along the wide, straight roads of Scarborough. He turned on the radio to the Top 40 station and rested one arm on the open window, a tanned arm with fine hairs that looked gold in the sunlight. I reached for my camera and pointed it out the window and snapped a picture as if with one shot I could capture all the plazas and apartments and driveways and houses, the rational layout of everything.

Craig parked at the far edge of the huge lot at the subway station, away from cars left by morning commuters. We sat in his mom's Pinto, surrounded by asphalt, the radio playing familiar songs, and we passed the mickey back and forth until it was empty. When he turned the radio off, neither of us said a thing to fill the silence. I didn't get out and he didn't start the engine. We were going to stay there until we figured something out about each other. We had the rest of the afternoon, probably the whole evening too.

I turned to Craig and looked at him through my camera. He grinned back and I took his picture. Then he looked away and his expression got serious and I took another, this time moving the camera so that later in my darkroom he would appear on paper as a mysterious blur.

NIGHT OF
THE POLAR FLEECE

———

Despite the distracting noise and glow of their computers and televisions and microwaves and refrigerators and tablets, the citizens of the city were inspired by the eco-guru's message to gather—collectively, simultaneously, momentously—at the windows of their homes to peer out past their night-darkened Hummers and up, up, up into the sky to seek out...the moon! And part of their minds pondered the possible relevance of this distant white sphere to their lives while another part— the part that normally waited to be fed the next media-generated image—longed to go check what was coming on TV at 9 pm. Would the eco-guru's message be heeded this moonlit evening as civilization spiralled toward environmental disaster?

I lowered my notebook, face burning. It was the first time I'd shared my apocalyptic prose, a recent effort. I was hoping to express my environmental consciousness through fiction.

"Well?" I asked Benny.

"Thought-provoking," he said, scratching his arm. Dry skin in the winter was a problem for him. "You're right about the moon, though. You hardly see the thing. You just forget it's still there."

"But do you like the *story*?"

The phone rang and he sprang for it.

It was Carson, our twelve-year-old, who was away skiing with a friend's family. They'd decided to stay another night to wait out the weather. I glanced outside. The snow was still coming down. It had been snowing full blast for days.

"Carson's conflicted," Benny said when he'd hung up. "The Walkers are planning to take him tonight to the resort's outdoor swimming pool and hot tub."

"Poor Carson. Maybe he can tweet about what a disgusting waste of energy that is. Get over the guilt that way."

"Actually, he said he's going to wait for them in the lobby. In other news, I need to get the car to the dealership for a tune-up before they close."

"In a snowstorm?"

"Barb, it's a short drive. What could happen?" He tossed the car keys up and caught them. "Listen, I'll get takeout on the way back and then we can have a quiet evening, *just us two*."

The economy was tanking, along with Benny's hockey-equipment business, now in receivership. He was sending his resumé to big-box stores he'd previously despised and I was smiling supportively until my cheeks ached. I bit my tongue about perilous road conditions rather than undermine his confidence.

After he left I got out the polar fleece outfits I'd made for us to wear around the house. Now we could keep the thermostat at its lowest setting. I spread the three outfits across the couch: Benny's, Carson's, mine. They were electric blue, but since we'd only wear them inside, what did it matter? It had been a struggle convincing Carson to try his on. Their neck-to-toe design did resemble baby pyjamas, but would effectively trap body heat. Carson had forgotten to pack his for the ski trip, which left me with a feeling of foreboding. I stepped into mine and reached down to zip up. I pulled on high boots and a long coat and headed out to shovel, pocketing my cell for good measure.

I'd cleared the snow earlier but again it was knee-deep. Along the driveways and sidewalks, piles stood shoulder-height. Relentless and ridiculous, the snow threatened to bring the city to a standstill. Benny had managed to get the car down the street, but I still worried. More snow was falling, occasionally blowing horizontally in rogue gusts from a tormented mauve sky now deepening into another interminable winter night. Up on the hydro wires beside a small transformer was a hunched-up squirrel. Only, this squirrel was still. It didn't budge. It didn't budge, I realized, because it had been electrocuted into a creepy tableau of its last moment. Despite the warmth of my fleece, I shivered. I dug the shovel into the snow even as more of it hurtled down at me. If I stood still, I'd disappear.

My pocket rang.

"Bad news," Benny said. "I hit a bishop."

"My god! You hit someone?"

"Actually, I hit a *car* with a bishop *in it*. Everyone's okay. It was all in slow-mo."

"But a *bishop*?"

"The guy's friend called him Bishop Castello. He's old and he's wearing black. I'm trying to be respectful here."

"This is terrible. What should I do?" The snow kept falling, dumb wet flakes smacking my face.

"Relax. We're waiting for the police. I'm just letting you know I'm delayed."

I finished clearing the sidewalk, shaky with worry and exhaustion and hunger. When I tried to open the door, it wouldn't. I'd accidentally shut it with the lock engaged. I didn't have the key. Most of my neighbours' homes were dark. Not yet back from work, likely delayed by the storm. One house had lights on but I'd recently alienated them by extracting unrecyclables from their bins and leaving them on their doormat. In my pocket I found a toonie. A ticket to a slice of pizza on the Danforth. Which would kill time until Benny returned.

Only a few sections of sidewalk were cleared. People had just given up. I trudged along a rutted tire track on the deserted road. Lit by the street lamps, the snowflakes looked too huge, too sparkly, like chunks of plastic. The Danforth was quiet too. The snowfall had discouraged most drivers and slowed the ones still out. Stores had closed early.

At Pizza-Yeah! I bought a vegetarian slice. The only customer, I sat by the window and ate tiny, time-wasting bites, chewing slowly. The pizza guy kept staring out the window, ignoring the TV news about troop deployment in some distant desert. The heat of the oven was unbearable.

I dialled Benny.

"The damage was minor," he said. "Now the car has another reason to be here at the dealership—so *two* birds! I'm waiting for the courtesy van. I'll be home soon."

"But now *I'm* not home. I'm locked out. Call me when you get back."

"Roger, baby." He made kissy noises. Being unemployed was making him extra amorous.

Pizza slice consumed, the library seemed the logical next destination. I was headed there when I heard a gasp on the snow-choked sidewalk. A woman in a white coat and purple wool hat with an enormous pompom stood in front of me.

"Winter!" she shouted. "Magical!"

I squinted through snowflakes to see her better. She had the thrilled look that dogs get hanging out car windows, feeling the wind on their eyeballs. It isn't winter *per se* that troubles me—my ice skates are sharpened and at the ready, my toboggan always game for action. What frightens are the extremes of our newly distorted climate. What irks is people cheerily cultivating their nature-sabotaging lifestyles. I contemplated bringing these issues to her attention, but my cell rang.

"Bit of a snag, Barb. I'm in North York."

"What?" I wailed.

"Is everything okay?" the woman asked.

"Who's that?" Benny asked.

"Never mind. Just tell me what's going on."

"The courtesy van had three of us to drop off and two were headed uptown. I didn't realize until we were already rolling. It's not so bad, though. Patrick here is a financial advisor so he's giving me excellent tips."

"This is crazy, Benny! You'll never get home."

"Is everything okay?" the woman asked.

"Who the *hell* is that talking?" Benny said.

It was exactly then that the street lights and the store lights flickered and everything plugged in went dark.

"Oh, great. A power out, Benny. Can you believe this?"

"Here too," he said. "It's completely dark."

My rib cage seemed to shrink, squeezing the air from my lungs. "Benny, Benny, Benny!" I whimpered.

"Deep breaths, Barb. It's just a blackout. Let me see—didn't you say blackouts mean we follow Emergency Plan D—"

Over the pounding of blood in my ears, I heard shocked exclamations in the background of the call.

"Barb, it seems like the—" and the cell went dead.

"Oh my god!" the woman said, face tilted skyward. I'd forgotten she was there. "It's as dark as the countryside gets. Where there's absolutely nothing around. This is just so incredibly beautiful."

"Are you fucking nuts? It's an *emergency*."

The first sirens sounded in the distance, followed by voices as people emerged from buildings. Emergency Plan D meant returning home, but I couldn't get in and now Benny was stuck too. I had to believe Carson wasn't affected. I had no idea what to do.

"I was headed there." The woman pointed to a narrow storefront in the gloom ahead. "I'll bet they have candles. And booze." She looked up again. "Too bad we're missing tonight's full moon."

Panicked and disoriented, I was now stepping through the snow alongside her. She stopped at a door with a sign that glowed in the dark: The Lucid Café.

"You coming in?" she asked.

Reassured by her kind smile and needing somewhere warm to regroup, I followed her.

"Power's out!" a high-pitched male voice called out. "Poetry reading's cancelled. We're closed."

"It's me, Geraldine," the woman said. "And a friend." She turned to me, lowering her voice. "Pretend you're a writer."

"In fact, I am," I said, surprised at the feeling of homecoming.

"Both writers," she sang in falsetto.

"Lock the door after you," came another voice. "Don't want any crazies walking in."

The room was narrow with darkly painted walls and a bar along one side. We settled ourselves among the half-dozen people sitting around several tables that were pushed together and lit with candles. The room had a dreamy feel. Warm and dreamy. Very warm.

Someone emerged from the bar and brought us two cups of wine.

"We're discussing the literary value of snowstorms," a bearded man whispered to Geraldine.

"Whatever we *were* discussing," a terse young woman said, "we need to start paying attention to what's next. I mean, first it's the storm, now the power's out. It could get bad."

"It might be city-wide," I offered. "It's off in North York too. And my cellphone isn't working."

A couple of people pulled theirs out.

"No reception," a woman said. "Freaky."

"Land line should be fine."

"Not this one," the guy at the bar said.

"Then it's just us tonight," someone said, "completely isolated from the rest of the world with only our unpublished words to guide us."

"Now, *that* is frightening!"

A few people laughed.

"Is this really the time to be clowning?" asked the terse woman.

"It's kind of toasty in here!" Geraldine took her coat off.

"I cranked the heat earlier," the bar guy said. "Should last a few hours."

I was boiling but determined to keep my special garment under wraps.

A large man walked to the front window and craned his neck, surveying the conditions outside. "Now what?" he asked.

"Safer to stay put."

"Shit, I'm worried about my cats," someone said.

"I'm worried about my kids," said Geraldine. "They're with the sitter, but still. I hope they know where the flashlight is."

The bar guy tapped a glass for attention. "Okay, everyone. Let's just calm the nerves. A toast to the resourcefulness of our families and pets. All shall be well. Transformers shall be repaired."

Lightning flashed, followed by a rumble of thunder.

"What the hell?" the large man said.

"Thundersnow," I explained. "Electrical storms can occur during snowstorms."

"Thor beckons us," the barman said.

"It's the Thunderbird beating its huge wings," said Geraldine. "Who is wrathful for some reason."

"It's global fucking warming," the terse woman said. "Mother Nature's revenge."

"Yo, Cass. Lighten up."

"Back to the toast? To all being well?"

Everyone swigged in unison.

"Enough of disasters," the large man said. "Let's talk about our writing."

"What are you working on?" Geraldine asked, turning to me.

"A short story," I said, as if offering an old sandwich from my purse: something with little value, possibly repellant.

"What about?" the bearded man asked.

"Society's disconnection from natural processes and the resulting impact of a degraded environment. That's the larger theme. There are sub-themes." I was finally realizing what my story was about. I wanted to grab pen and paper and let my mind run free.

"Oh boy," the bar guy said. "Not sure that's a good subject for fiction."

"No, hey, c'mon, c'mon." The large man returned to the table. "It could work."

I was burning up. The heat, the wine, the stress. I bravely unzipped my coat.

"Better, perhaps, not to dwell on the big depressing picture," said a tiny fellow in the corner who'd been quiet until then. "A Chinese poet, who lived about sixteen hundred years ago, said it well:

Wine I poured out for my guests
Wine we pressed on each other
Who knows
If ever the occasion would return.
Wine-flushed, the here and now we transcended,
Forgetting the cares of a thousand years
Come what may tomorrow,
Drink up I shall the pleasures of this day."

Without a word we clutched our cups and gulped.

A few hazy moments later, Geraldine craned her neck over the table, staring at me. "That looks like a cozy sweater—uh, pantsuit."

The blue glowed phosphorescent.

"It's for cold days. I made it."

"It's adorable," she purred.

"Do you take orders?" asked the tiny fellow. "It's freezing in my house when I get up early to write."

"I hadn't thought of the commercial possibilities," I said, thinking of the commercial possibilities. Which reminded me about Benny, stuck in North York, his business recently failed. I'd had enough wine and thought I should see if Benny or any of my neighbours had made it home. I exchanged e-mail addresses with the group and was asked to read at their next event in lieu of paying my part of the tab. Cass headed out too.

Outside was still dark but the snow had let up. The sky was starting to clear, and the moon, full that night, gave some of its light from behind a thin cloud. I was about to say goodbye to

Cass when I remembered where I'd seen her.

"Don't you work at the deli counter in Ultra-Store?"

"I quit," she said. "It was frying my brain."

"Maybe you should write about your experiences there."

She snorted. "Anyway, good luck with your story. Go for it. Don't listen to them. Write whatever you want." She kicked the snow in front of her. "It's Armageddon out here."

Maybe the wine had blotted out earlier fears of ending up alone on a dark street with snow-obliterated buildings, but now the blackout seemed less dire, maybe just a chance to experience natural darkness, the night laid bare. An adventure, even. Like this chance meeting with a group of writers.

"It's almost spring," I said. "That always makes me hopeful."

Cass shrugged and waved over her shoulder as she walked away.

I headed home, each step a struggle through the snow. My street had a charming old-world vibe with candle-lit windows and the gently shifting shadows of neighbours spending time together without electronic distractions. As I approached our house I kept my fingers crossed.

Benny was out on the porch wearing nothing but his blue fleece outfit and a white toque.

"Benny! You're home!"

"I was worried sick about you!" he said, hustling me inside and taking off my coat.

"What about Carson? How can we reach him?"

"Our land line's working. He's fine. He ended up in that crazy outdoor pool, snowstorm be damned. He said something about everyone needing the occasional break from being the change they want to see in the world. He said you taught him that."

"How depressing. This world is screwed." I kicked off my boots.

"C'mon, Barb, lighten up." He nuzzled me, and the friction of polyester against polyester caused a spark. "Wow," he said, "we can make our *own* electricity."

"We'll need to if things continue to decline. What are we going to do?"

"We're going to let nature take her course," Benny murmured. His nose was in my hair, his hands exploring my fleece-covered hills and valleys. He wouldn't lay off. I put my hand against Benny's chest to hold him back and felt the softness of the fabric and also his wildly thumping heart. We had each other, at least.

Over his shoulder I could see the glow of the full moon.

"Come what may tomorrow," I recited. *"Drink up I shall the pleasures of this day."*

"That a line from your story, Barb-bunny?" His hands were zeroing in on vital regions. The temperature was suddenly warmer than a climate change-induced heat alert. Only it felt great.

"Forget my story," I said. I reached for his zipper. Then pulled the tab down and him along with it.

GHOST WOMAN

———

THE AFTERNOON TV NEWS shows a lane between the walls of a church and an old brick house. With snow piled against a chain-link fence at the end, it looks like just another cold place in a cold city. But Cheung sits forward on the couch to see better, trying to follow the reporter's fast flow of words. He knows this place: it's just around the corner from the apartment where he and his daughter live. The night before, long after midnight, he passed by and in it he saw a woman standing alone.

He wants to ask Lillian to translate but she's reading a fashion magazine in the armchair, Walkman headphones on, even though she switched the channel from the Cantonese one. She wears a tight sleeveless T-shirt, black bra strap against her naked shoulder. "Just a style," she said when he complained it was not what her mother would have allowed. The news anchor is back on the screen, accompanied by a photo of a young blond woman. Cheung understands enough to learn she has something to do with the lane. And then he realizes the woman was found dead.

The news moves on to a story about the world's computers, a problem about the approaching millennium that Lillian keeps mentioning, but he isn't listening. His thoughts spin around the image of the woman. He gets up, wills himself to forget. Tomorrow is the first day of Chinese New Year and dark thoughts could poison his luck. He needs all the luck he can get for the coming year, their third in Canada, with the rumour now of a layoff at work.

From the kitchen he calls her. Without turning, she lifts the headphones off one ear.

"I'll make noodles for lunch," he says. "Then we can go to Zellers." He is pleased she agreed to go shopping with him. The tradition was to buy a new outfit. New clothes for a new year. A fresh start.

"No, Daddy, I can't anymore. I'm leaving in a minute. I'm seeing a movie with my friends."

Lillian, jiggling her foot, returns to her reading. He considers pleading with her but decides not to risk her scorn or an argument that might spill into the New Year. This rudeness worries him, as does the tight clothing and the black-rimmed eyes and painted nails. He is grateful that she does well at school, even with her recent habit of going out evenings with friends. On those nights he puts on the TV just to have noise in the apartment, telling himself she is safe and behaving well, while he sits on the couch, tired from another day of hammering or painting or lifting, and watches the screen but drifts to sleep. And into dreams that take him back to Hong Kong and to May, and when the howling winter wind startles him awake and Lillian is still not home, he feels as empty as the frozen street outside the window.

Cheung half-fills the wok with water and sets it on the burner. From the cupboard he takes ramen noodles and eggs from the fridge. He doesn't cook well, just basic meals. He straightens the dishtowel, waiting for the water to boil, hoping Lillian will change her mind and eat with him. Does she still remember the elaborate feast her mother prepared each New Year's Eve? Tofu with minced pork, fish, three different vegetable dishes, beef, a whole steamed chicken.

"Don't be late home," he says. "We will go for dinner at six."

"I might not be back in time. Can't you go join Tak's family?"

His cousin, their only relative in Toronto, didn't invite them to their house this year. Tonight Cheung planned to take Lillian to Gold Fortune down the street. If she doesn't show up, he will eat in the apartment alone.

Not long before May died she finally said aloud what Cheung had been thinking but could not bring himself to say aloud: she should have the photograph taken. She didn't need to explain what photograph she meant.

Her fate was to die at thirty-nine. That was how things sometimes went. Everyone died eventually; the unlucky died young. These simple facts helped him during those first weeks of tasks and obligations. They helped again on his last day in Hong Kong as he crouched on the cemetery pavement. Her grave was one of thousands of upright granite tombstones set side by side in terraced rows up the mountain, a regiment of the dead bordered by concrete walkways that the sun turned a blinding white. On each stone was a photograph. He avoided looking at May's as he burned the ceremonial money and incense. He arranged the cake and barbecued pork on a plastic plate, and beside it placed a thermos and small cup that he filled with tea. He stood up and held the incense, bowing three times like his mother had taught him to do for his father years earlier. And when she died the year before, he had done it for her too. Honour the gods. Provide for your loved one in the afterlife. Your ancestors are your foundation. Be respectful and careful when dealing with the dead. He wasn't convinced there was another world to step into after this one, but these small rituals eased his mind.

After burning the offerings, he swept the ashes and packed the food away. In the bay below, the water looked green and still. He lit a cigarette. He was not the type to make detailed plans or put things on paper, but lately that's all he'd been doing. He'd completed May's government and insurance documents, then revised his and Lillian's Canadian immigration applications. He'd spent hours waiting to talk to various officials through slots in glass barriers. It was 1995, two years before the communist takeover of Hong Kong, and everyone was nervous, wanting to leave. Many were going to Canada. At the market and in the restaurants he overheard discussions about the best Chinatowns, about which cities had tolerable winters, everyone pretending to have special insight. It was agreed that wherever you ended up would be dull compared to Hong Kong. Older people bought bags of rice and dried mushrooms to bring along, not trusting the stores in those distant cities.

Finally Cheung's application was approved. For Lillian's sake he was relieved but it came too late for May, whose remains he was reluctant to leave. Only now did he realize he would be the first in his family to leave the region of his ancestors. But he found comfort in the congratulations from his friends and neighbours. When he shared his good news the pity left their eyes.

He turned again toward May's grave, finally ready to look at her photograph. With hair pulled back, mouth closed, eyes cold, she confronted the camera that forced her to acknowledge what was going to happen. But now she looked at Cheung too and something about her eyes appeared to soften. From wherever she was, she looked out at him, alive and about to leave her, both pleased and sad. He said his goodbye to this black and white image of May, taken instead of a passport photo.

At first Cheung and Lillian stayed with his cousin in Markham. But living in the suburbs required a car, something he couldn't afford. When he learned there was a Chinatown in the east end of Toronto, near to streetcars and the subway, he rented a second-floor flat above a bakery. On this strip of Gerrard Street, and at the nearby mall, he could buy what he needed and speak Cantonese. The food wasn't as good as in Hong Kong and the pace of life was slow, but they were safe now from the Chinese government.

He called his cousin's friend and got a job with a small construction company. He would no longer be a taxi driver, at least not until his English improved and he'd saved enough money. At forty-five, he would start again, learn what he could about drywall and paint, work as many hours as he could get.

As the months passed, Lillian made friends and talked less often about her mother, even as she grew to resemble her more. The shopkeepers gave her sweet bean buns and watched over her. Especially Cecelia Wu in the stationery shop, who laughed gamely at Cheung's awkward attempts to get to know her. He felt disloyal to May while checking Cecelia's figure as she tidied the shelves and asked him about life back home. One evening he saw a fashionable man waiting for her to lock up and felt foolish for believing she would ever take him seriously.

By late August Toronto was as hot as Hong Kong, but the many trees and gardens sweetened the air. He asked the bakery owner where to enroll Lillian in school. When they found the building, he handed the secretary a piece of paper with their address and phone number. Lillian did all the talking. He watched her small face, a near likeness of May's, as she concentrated on the secretary's questions. She would improve her English inside that building. Then she could teach him, just like May had made her promise. At least he had Lillian, as clever as her mother, a good daughter who understood and even liked this strange new place.

He first saw May in his Tai Koo neighbourhood. She was a waitress in a small noodle restaurant where she handled the heat and pressure of the busy lunch hours with grace, whisking between tables, heavy platters balanced on slim arms. She didn't respond to the teasing comments about her long swinging braid or the compliments offered by the other men who were just as delighted as Cheung to find her in that hovel. But if asked about the food, she would eagerly recommend the freshest dishes. Her serious expression made her seem mature and wise. She studied business part-time at the university, she revealed to him one lunch when she returned his smile and paused at his table. She supported herself and the aunt she lived with. Here was a woman who valued hard work.

Cheung worked hard himself, driving his taxi every day. He lived with his parents but was saving for an apartment, barely concerned about the Chinese takeover, then still over a dozen years away. Though people were already applying to emigrate, few wanted to leave Hong Kong with its mountain parks and streets alive at all hours with people, where you didn't feel alone. He and May strolled one of the crowded sidewalks on that first afternoon together, when she agreed to join him for tea.

It was the largest home Cheung had ever been in. At the end of a curved road lined with wide driveways but no visible cars or people sat a tall brick house with white columns and double front doors. Inside, Jimmy Cho, the foreman, led the crew up the curved staircase to a bedroom that was bigger than Cheung and Lillian's apartment. They'd be enlarging the bathroom, Jimmy said, before taking a call on his cell. Cheung and Mak looked around while they waited for instructions. The matching furniture, patterned fabrics and dark walls made the room feel heavy and inevitable, as if their tools could not possibly alter it. The tall windows had silvery curtains that skimmed the polished wood floor. He wondered how this Canadian family had made their money. People from Hong Kong prospered in Canada too but were either educated or rich already, or still young, like the guys he worked with, who talked about starting their own business one day and buying a house. Cheung was barely covering his expenses. He was determined not to touch the modest savings he'd brought, money to help with Lillian's education and some left for his old age.

Jimmy finished his call and told them to start shifting furniture away from the wall they would be removing.

"Careful, careful," he kept saying. They shuffled lamps and a small table to the other side of the room. Mak pointed to a large wood dresser. He and Cheung positioned themselves at either end, but it wouldn't budge. They shifted to the front and started removing drawers. The first one Cheung slid out held colourful bras and panties, a garden of purples, pinks, and reds.

Mak whistled. "She's hot, this rich *gweipo*." He dipped his finger in and lifted a scarlet bra. With his other hand he clutched his crotch in mock ecstasy.

Cheung smiled, more at the Cantonese slang. Ghost woman. That and *gweilo*, ghost man, what everyone called the white foreigners in Hong Kong, who they'd see occasionally in the clamour of a neighbourhood market looking lost.

"Hey!" Jimmy shouted. "Leave the owner's stuff alone. You want to get me in trouble?"

"Wish my wife wore things like that," Mak said, and slid a

different drawer out, this one with folded sweaters. He carried it over to where they were stacking everything.

Cheung moved the drawer of lingerie without touching any of it. May hadn't worn this sort of thing either, but he hadn't cared. Her naked skin was enough for him. Especially during those first months of warm evenings in his bed. When they found out she was pregnant, the decision to marry had been easy. They would build a stable life together.

Cheung carried the last drawer over to the others and noticed a photo on the bedside table. A family portrait: the woman who lived here smiling confidently, surrounded by her husband and children. Cheung imagined her sleeping peacefully at night in this perfect room and a wave of bitterness overcame him. When no one was looking, he put the picture face down.

The night Cheung saw the woman in the lane was the coldest that winter. Walking south on Broadview from the subway, he felt the icy wind lash his face. His coat was thick and heavy but still not enough to keep him warm. He regretted not waiting inside the station for the streetcar. It was already past midnight and his mind felt hazy from too much beer as he headed home from a full day's work followed by the company's New Year dinner. The food had been good but there'd been hints of a possible layoff. The oldest and least skilled of the crew, he'd be the first to go.

Through the long meal, his glass had been continually refilled. Jimmy and Mak, downing cognac as well, shouted and poked fun at each other. Cheung enjoyed the chance to relax and the reminder of New Years in Hong Kong where for ten days everyone stopped working to celebrate and the city was festive with displays of flowers and cherry-blossom branches, with red and gold decorations and strings of lights. By day people visited friends and family, then filled the streets at night to shop and stroll and watch the fireworks.

He reached the stretch of Broadview that curved along the top of the valley, its view of the downtown skyline offering a bit of cheer in the forbidding night. How strange for him to walk here alone in darkness while at this very moment Hong Kong was sunny and deep into the next busy day. And somewhere in it lingered the spirit of his old life, what he and May had done and said and felt—still there, but fading. He remembered speeding home at the end of his shifts, energized by the sidewalk markets and crowds and the scent of frying meat, by radio voices spilling from open windows, a salty breeze from the South China Sea. Along this part of Broadview the wind swept unchecked and cold across the valley toward him. He crossed to the east side with its large brick homes, the yellow of the light in their windows suggesting warmth out of reach.

As he passed the lane beside a church, something moved at the far end. He slowed and saw a *gweipo* standing there, her skin pale and blue under the sky's dim light. Her breath rose in clouds through frigid air. Her coat only half-covered legs that were bare above her boots. The way she stood was odd, knees slightly bent, hands out, as if steadying herself. He hesitated. He tried to concentrate despite fatigue and the blur from drinking. She stared toward him and was still. Her voice, a loud whisper, was a surprise. He didn't catch the words. "You are okay?" he called back. She looked over her shoulder into the shadows. Was someone else there? She seemed to be waiting—but for what? Was it some kind of joke? She could be smiling. It was too dark. Fear propelled him along the sidewalk, quickly now, almost at a run, straining to listen above the pounding of blood in his head for the sound of footsteps.

He reached Gerrard before daring to look back. No one. Turning the corner, he rushed past Wong's closed grocery store, past empty crates and folded cardboard out for recycling, past the stationery shop's red decorations with their wishes for good luck in the New Year. Finally, his door. By the time he was climbing the steps to the apartment he began to believe he'd imagined the woman's voice and even the woman herself.

The disease hid in May during months of appointments and tests. He'd wake early each morning and watch her sleep. Nothing could be wrong with this body he loved to hold. He stared at her smooth shoulder and long neck, and at the faint sunspots on her face—the only hint of approaching middle age. Soon enough she lost weight and her skin turned sallow, the disease openly mocking their plans for the future, even the chance to see Lillian through to adulthood. May refused to discuss it. "Stop behaving like I'm made of glass," she said. "Treat me normally. Please." Each morning, his eyes flashed open before she woke so he could look at her while it was still possible.

May got sicker while Lillian slipped from childhood, dancing across the apartment to pop music. May fixated on tracking the status of their immigration application and planned what they would ship to Canada. They would hear soon. Their chances were good with her years of bookkeeping experience. She'd never finished university after Lillian was born, but her English was excellent. She talked about the plane ride that would carry them to a new life as if cancer was something they could simply leave behind.

The water is coming to a boil when Cheung hears Lillian, still sprawled in the chair, laugh at something on the television. The volume is turned up. English words shout from the living room.

That woman in the lane did not call for help: she had whispered something. She may have been frightened but he was frightened too, of trouble. Another thing he couldn't manage. If he'd gone closer and found out what she wanted, he would have only made things worse, unable to understand. Or he could have been the one attacked and then what would happen to Lillian? He did the right thing. That woman's troubles had nothing to do with him. He has troubles of his own.

The water in the wok is boiling. He stares at the surface, churning and rolling to the rhythm of the television's shouting words. What is Lillian becoming? She doesn't listen to him, cares more about her friends than a father who does everything for her good, her future. How could she dare to abandon him like this, leave him to eat alone for the year's most important dinner? May should still be alive. Here to guide their daughter. Here to help him in this freezing place she convinced him to come to. How could she let this happen? He strikes the cupboard with one fist and cries out her name. He shouts it again, only louder.

The living room goes quiet. Then comes Lillian's voice: "Daddy?"

Cheung hits the cupboard as if to rid his mind of that pale ghostly face. A woman in a lane. A criminal, a drug addict, a prostitute he had every reason to get away from. His arm, strong now from endless hours of physical work, swings again through the air and this time strikes the wok. The wok skids off the stove, crashing to the floor, but the boiling water flies up, splashing the calendar on the fridge, splashing the cupboards, splashing into the doorway where she appears, this strange and unknowable version of May, this woman in a tight shirt, black bra straps rude against bare skin, speaking English to everyone but him. This stranger's face with black-rimmed eyes now wide as the water burns her arms and hands, this stranger's scream, shrill and unending, that makes him scream along with her.

CLOSER

EUGENE DUG INTO THE BOX of Shannon's CDs and dropped a few from the second-floor window. He leaned out into the shock of January air and watched the cases crack open on the patio, discs whizzing across the frozen grass. He'd been doing this in the months since Shannon had left, taking their six-year-old daughter, Nellie. He looked into the box at the popular music Shannon listened to over the years of their marriage. He thought of dropping the discs as a way to mark his progression to whatever lay ahead. Every so often, he'd feel ready to drop some more. But he didn't want the box to be empty. Not yet. Downstairs, the house was quiet. The Chinese undergrads who rented the ground floor were probably out. He glanced at the clock. It was time to pick up his new driving student, who lived nearby.

He drove the few blocks from his house with Joy Division blaring. Lately, he was gravitating to music he'd listened to in his twenties, reconfiguring himself post-Shannon, or maybe it was regressing. He pulled up to the address, turned the stereo off, and checked the name on his clipboard: Laura Hanson. On the porch a woman was locking the front door. He got out to introduce himself, despite a temptation to just wave from the warmth of his seat. He recognized her. The other week he'd seen her bundled up in the same black coat and leaning into the wind, Valu-mart bags batting against her legs, her long brown hair like Shannon's, only pulled back. She walked over to the car, hands out as she navigated the icy concrete. When she glanced up, it was with a smile more wary than shy.

"Laura? Hi there, I'm Eugene. Here, why don't you take the passenger seat to start." He opened the door and she ducked in.

He got back in and turned to her. "I've seen you before. I live nearby." She looked a little washed-out up close, wearing no makeup.

"This isn't my house," she said, and hesitated. "I'm just looking after it for a friend while she's away. I live in Kingston."

"Welcome to Toronto, then." As he pulled away from the curb, he tried to think of something to ease the tension older students were prone to, being either new to the country or finally dealing with something long avoided. "So you signed up for four two-hour lessons—what I call the 'let's get this over with quick' package. Need your licence for work?"

"A kind of tour, actually."

"Tour?" Someone tried to cut him off and he tapped the horn. "Tour of what?"

"Glenn Gould. Places in his life."

"Okay, now that's original. You must be a big fan."

"In a way."

"You play piano?"

She didn't respond, and when he glanced over, she was just looking down.

"*I* played," Eugene said. "Took lessons when I was a kid." He grimaced, remembering his hours on that slippery wood bench. "I was lousy, though. I picked up an electric guitar in my teens. Was in a band with my friends. I still sucked but it didn't matter. New Wave: that's kind of what we aimed for."

He checked and she was looking at him.

"But that's good," she said. "You went back to music again, even when the first try didn't work."

"I never thought about it that way," he said.

"I was wondering something. Would it be possible to drive to some Gould sites during my lessons? Would that work?"

"I can see you're eager to be mobile—which is the right attitude—but let's start with the basics. Gas pedal, brake and all that. Okay?" Too late he realized he sounded sarcastic, a habit he'd slipped into to amuse himself with humourless students. "I'll drive us over to the lot at Ted Reeve Arena and get you in the driver's seat where you belong."

They arrived and switched places and when he asked her to park, she pulled smoothly into a spot, turning the steering wheel hand over hand. Pulling back out, she slid her arm behind his seat and looked over her shoulder.

"I'm guessing somebody's driven before."

"It's been a few years. I'd been close to getting my licence."

Eugene considered her request to visit the Gould sites. Why pass up an opportunity to make things more interesting? "Okay," he said. "Let's give your tour idea a try. What's up first?"

"Thirty-two Southwood Drive." She was smiling. "Where he grew up."

"It's nearby. I know the house. Plaque on the front lawn." Eugene stretched his legs, careful not to touch his instructor's brake, hoping this change of routine would be entertaining. He liked the rhythm of conversation during lessons, the faux-intimacy of time spent beside a stranger in a small vehicle. It was an antidote to the depressive suction of his personal life. "So, Laura, what *did* get you so keen on Mr. Gould?"

She kept driving down Main Street. "My son," she said finally.

"He's a musician?"

"A pianist."

Laura parked on the street in front of Gould's childhood home, a dark brick house, nondescript. She approached the plaque, Eugene following.

"So your son, is he another musical genius?"

"He was good. Very good." She put her hand out and touched the plaque. "I appreciate your interest, you know. But I'd rather not get into it." A streak of sun reached them through the trees. She squinted up at him. "Sorry."

"No, I'm sorry. I didn't mean to pry." Eugene followed her back to the car without another word.

Laura asked how to get to Malvern, the high school Gould attended, then drove in silence. Eugene leaned back. Another hour of circling the neighbourhood with this woman obsessed with a dead pianist, then his next student, the nervous Ethiopian who would blather about the restaurant he planned to open. After him, the sixteen-year-old with cologne that made him sneeze.

Shannon stood beside Eugene's couch. She'd just unpacked Nellie's weekend clothes, leaving them in a neat pile before drifting over to the box at the window. He half hoped she would look out and see the CDs, visible in the snow. He wouldn't have minded hearing what she thought was wrong with him if it meant she'd stay longer. He liked it when she lingered like this, especially for the reward after she left, her scent in the room and the memories it inspired.

"Why are you still keeping these CDs separate? If you don't like them, get rid of them."

"I thought you might change your mind and take them after all." But he knew she wouldn't. The townhouse she'd just bought and filled with new furnishings lacked any reminders of her former life with him. "Maybe," he added, "I'm not as good as you at throwing away the past."

"I'm not going into that again. It's caustic. And completely inappropriate around Nellie."

From the next room came a sudden creak. Through the doorway they saw their daughter's white stockings as she rebounded from a plunge onto the bed, the bed they'd conceived her on. Eugene wondered if Shannon was thinking this too.

"What's inappropriate for Nellie is her parents separating." He said this noticing Shannon's breasts, which he still had trouble accepting as permanently off limits or, worse, new territory for some other pair of hands. How would he know if she was seeing someone?

"God, Eugene, what is up with you?"

"In mourning, I guess." He sank into the couch and stared up at the ceiling.

"I still say: make some changes in your life. Get a better job. Pull yourself out of this funk."

"This fucking funk of mine." Eugene kept his voice low. According to Shannon, Eugene's problem was lack of ambition. The proof being his decision to fall back on his driving instruction credentials after the bank laid him off five years before. Shannon had still been home with Nellie and, financially, it was all up to him. But he'd had it with the corporate world.

He'd made his case to her: being an instructor covered their costs if they lived modestly and gave him flexibility to be home part of the day to help with Nellie. And he made decent extra income buying and selling stocks on the Net. For a while it was okay, until Shannon got restless and returned to the marketing sector, working late, taking courses to upgrade her skills. It paid off in promotions and invitations to parties that gave her the money and excuse to buy pricey clothes. With Nellie starting Grade 1 came Shannon's campaign to move to a more affluent school district. He'd dug in his heels and what had been unravelling came undone.

She moved away from the window and looked at Eugene on the couch. "All I'm saying is you're worthy of more." Her voice had softened.

Coming from Shannon, this remnant of concern was encouraging. It made him want to get sloppy with her over wine, tell her how he was trying to fill in all the chunks of time that used to be about family. He wanted to tell her that sometimes he looked for consolation in strange places, like when he'd driven to Loblaws, picked up a loaf of bread and lined up behind people with full carts while the question "Why not the express checkout?" twitched in everyone's smiles. The answer was in the cashier's name. He wanted to say hello to Hope, a cheerful older woman who always remembered him.

"Why don't you stay, Shannon? Have dinner with Nellie and me."

"Eugene, I have plans." She looked at him with the same weariness as when she'd finally said it flat out: *I'm just not in love anymore.*

Eugene parked and tapped the horn. He got out and walked around to the passenger side to wait, kicked a chunk of slushy ice from the mud flap, if only for the satisfaction of making something happen. It was a mild day and he hoped the light rain would wash the filth off his car. He used to be more diligent about keeping it clean.

Laura got into the driver's seat with the same composed expression as before. She didn't seem to wear makeup, but her blue eyes stood out and were difficult to look away from.

"So where's today's Gould hotspot?" he asked, noticing a pleasant shampoo-like scent.

"Massey Hall. I'm a bit nervous about traffic downtown but I'd like to also try driving to his statue. It's at the CBC building. If you think that would be okay?"

"You're the boss. Mirror adjustments and we're off."

Rain darkened the asphalt as she drove them along the Danforth. She put the windshield wipers on top speed and he decided to tolerate the frantic swishing as he looked out through the streaks of rain on the window. They passed the Petro Canada, with its yellowed evergreens, and the used-appliance store with a fridge on display in the window, and he felt acutely aware of the two of them, both apparently single, alone in his car together.

"So," Eugene said, "tell me about Massey Hall."

"That's where Gould played his first orchestral concert. He was only thirteen." She straightened up and continued, describing his life as a concert pianist in the 1950s. Then at mid-career he'd terminated all live appearances, something about hating crowds and air travel and a preference for the artistic control and solitude of the recording studio. She almost sounded like she was showing Gould off, like a mother would. He wondered what the parallels were to her son, what had happened to him, but didn't want to shut her down again by asking.

She took one hand off the wheel to tuck her hair behind her

ear and glanced at him. "Can you tell me where I should turn? I had the route figured out but I've forgotten this part."

He directed her the rest of the way and to a parking lot near the CBC building. Sitting on a bench outside was a life-size bronze Gould wearing an overcoat, cap and gloves. Laura sat beside it and examined the face, its expression of bemused self-consciousness. Eugene waited a few feet away, feeling like an interloper.

Finally she looked up. "This feels wrong. He wouldn't have sat here like this. It's too public. He was happiest being alone."

Eugene hesitated. Her eyes were glassy. He wanted to talk to her about being alone, about living temporarily in that house, no sign or mention of anyone else. Loneliness and winter. He could say a thing or two about trying to survive that duo. He checked his watch. He needed to pick up his next student soon. The light was waning, the cold creeping up his legs and down the collar of his coat, and he was thinking of the drink he'd have later at home. "We should probably head back," he said, "before traffic gets bad."

It was Eugene's weekend with Nellie. He was walking her to her friend's birthday party, a sleepover. At five-thirty it was dark already, the air sharp and clean. Nellie wore her Barbie knapsack and Eugene carried her pillow and sleeping bag under his arms. They'd had fun playing Monopoly all afternoon and now they were quiet, the crunch of their boots on the snow the only sound in their world. He thought about all the new people in her life—teachers, friends, a nanny—people he didn't know, and worried she was slipping away from him. With work clogging most afternoons and weekends, he could only be responsible for her on alternate Saturday nights and Sundays.

After dropping Nellie off he felt like walking and soon found himself on Laura's block, slowing as he neared her house. His breath rose in soft clouds toward a light in an upstairs window where he imagined piano music playing. Her shadow stretched across a wall as she crossed the room. Eugene looked away, kept walking.

At his house he headed down the driveway to the backyard, past the window of what used to be his study. The Chinese students were slouched inside watching TV. The dachshund next door started yapping, snout poked through the chain-link. Eugene felt around in the snow, hands freezing even with gloves. There might be some classical CDs, maybe a Gould. But all he found were club mixes. Dancing with Shannon, that flash in her eyes and the way she moved that had startled and excited him. How could he dismiss what they'd had together: ten better-than-decent years of lust and companionship? And a daughter he missed every day.

Upstairs, he considered looking up Gould on the internet. He hadn't listened to much classical before, though he liked it in movies—in the sad parts. But sad wasn't how he wanted to feel for the rest of the evening. He brought the duvet over to the couch, flicked the TV on and let some Scotch burn slowly down his throat.

The next day a winter storm paralyzed the city. Eugene cancelled his students, calling Laura last. Was it nervousness or a desire to look forward a little longer to her voice on the phone? It was an awkward call though. She sounded distant, concerned only about the weather, focused on getting through their scheduled lessons.

His car was encased in ice so he walked to the liquor store, gusts of snow pistol-whipping him. It was like the recent storm during Christmas, when Shannon had taken Nellie to Ottawa to see her mom and dad. His own parents were out in Victoria so he'd spent the holidays alone, and often drunk, pissed off at Shannon for changing things, for making him feel like a loser.

He finally got home through the storm. In the kitchen, he left the Scotch on the counter and made tea, then sat down at the computer and found a website with a black and white photo of Gould looking back at him. Eugene's thoughts drifted to Laura: her profile in his car, her pale hands on the steering wheel. Where would she take him next? Eugene clicked on the biography link and started reading.

Laura drove them along St. Clair, stopping in front of the apartment Gould lived in during the last two decades of his life. It took her half a dozen manoeuvres to park, leaving the car marooned over a foot from the curb. She walked toward the modest brick building while Eugene checked that the car wasn't in the way of passing traffic.

"We better work more on your parallel parking," he said, catching up to where she stood looking up at one of the windows.

"It was just a small apartment," she said, "filled with sheet music—and his grand piano, of course. He still made recordings and did radio and television work, but he was mostly wrapped up in himself, and it closed in on him a little. He almost couldn't handle it."

Eugene looked up too, trying to imagine this other man's world. "Couldn't handle what?"

"His own genius. His fear of illness, that something would happen to him. He kept detailed records of his blood pressure, sometimes hourly, took pills for everything, real and imagined. There was something about his brilliance that kept him from living properly."

"He died of a stroke, right?"

She nodded. Eugene looked east to Yonge where there were a couple of places to eat. "I don't have anyone else booked today. How about a coffee somewhere nearby?"

"It's too bad Fran's Restaurant isn't here anymore. That's where he used to eat."

"Where he ordered fried eggs," Eugene added, "in the middle of the night." He walked back toward the car, certain she'd be surprised and maybe pleased. "I'll put some money in the meter," he said.

Seated across from Laura, Eugene enjoyed the chance to look straight at her dark blue eyes. "You haven't said much about yourself. I mean, you've said a lot about Glenn Gould, but—"

"What do you expect me to say? You're my driving instructor." She took a sip of her coffee, frowning.

Why did she have to make conversation so awkward?

Eugene watched the waitress serve the next table. "It's just, I get the impression you're all on your own. I only say that," he added, "because I'm alone myself. My situation, recently, has been difficult. I have an ex-wife—a separated wife. What I mean is, a wife I'm separated from. And a young daughter."

"I can understand that would be difficult." Her eyes flicked briefly to his.

"I figured it should be getting easier, but it isn't yet. The way I'm feeling is: it's either up or down from here. Because straight ahead is taking the piss out of me."

"Maybe you should take a vacation," she said. Her face was expressionless.

He hoped she didn't mean it. He hoped she knew what crappy advice that was. "Travelling alone isn't very appealing."

Laura clasped her hands around her mug.

"You mentioned going to see Gould's grave," Eugene said. "But I guess it's getting late."

"Could we save that for next time? I'm tired. I'd like to go home."

It was almost dark when they got to the car. They put their seat belts on in silence, shivering as they waited for the heat to kick in. She fumbled with the switches, trying to locate the one for the headlights, and Eugene leaned over to show her—nothing more—and found himself pressing his face against her soft hair. She remained still for a moment, then gently pushed him away.

"I'm sorry. I didn't mean—" Eugene slouched against the car door.

Her voice was quiet. "You can't just do that."

"Of course. I don't know why—"

"Your problems, they have nothing to do with me."

"I know that. I'm sorry. I'm really sorry." Failed husband and father, he thought. Failed business grad too. And now, failed driving instructor. "We better get going."

Taking a deep breath, she signalled, checked her blind spot and joined the flow of cars. Eugene was still trying to process what he'd just done when she started talking.

"My son Jonathan played beautifully," she said. "He was no Gould but he might have had a concert career." She stopped for a few seconds, then continued. "The problem was he was nervous in competition."

A van signalled and began to cross into their lane. Laura didn't see, and accelerated, almost hitting it.

"Slow down!" Eugene's hand shot across to the steering wheel, his foot pressing his brake. "You didn't give the guy time to merge!"

She eased off the gas until she was way under the speed

limit. Another car honked and passed them.

"Are you okay?" Eugene asked. He felt a wave of anger at himself for not having seen that coming. "Turn left here at the light. *Carefully.*"

But she signalled right and pulled onto a quiet street. She stopped the car by the curb. Eugene waited for whatever she needed to say.

"By the time Jonathan was sixteen, he was ready to quit. He still idolized Gould, though. We talked about coming to Toronto and seeing all the landmarks. I thought it might lead to other options, like studying composing or maybe teaching. I started taking driving lessons. We couldn't afford a car. I was planning to rent one and take him on this tour." Laura kept staring straight ahead. "What's your daughter's name?"

He released a breath he hadn't realized he'd been holding. "Nellie. She's six."

Laura nodded, looking through the windshield as if at something she did not want to see.

It was late Sunday afternoon. Eugene was back home after spending the day with Nellie. He had talked about the two of them going up north for a few days. He'd rent a chalet and teach her to ski. She made him promise they'd really do it, and when he kissed her goodbye, it was the first time he'd felt okay about leaving her. He cooked himself a proper dinner and made a plan with some friends to watch the hockey game later in the week. It felt good making contact again. He should have called months earlier. Then he went to do what had been at the back of his mind all day. When he opened the window, cold air rushed in as if it had been waiting there all evening. He lifted the box out and turned it upside down. Outside, the dachshund started a new round of barking.

He sat down on the couch and thought about Laura. The next day was her last lesson.

The end of the tour was Mount Pleasant Cemetery. The drive there had consisted of tips for dealing with the test examiner, the usual stuff he doled out, though his mind churned with other things he wanted to say. He and Laura stood in front of the flat stone, engraved with the shape of a grand piano and the first notes of Gould's favourite Bach piece. Gould was only fifty when he died, just seven years older than Eugene. Around them, the stones darkened as the light left the sky. Eugene was anxious to be out of there, though not for Laura's time to end.

"Gould believed in a hereafter," she said. "What about you?"

"I'm not so sure about that. I guess I'm banking everything on this life, just in case."

"That's probably the right thing to do," she said, her voice wavering.

"You okay?"

"No, actually." She laughed and pulled a tissue from her pocket, pressing it to her eyes. He had to control an impulse to hug her.

"I don't know," he said, trying to sound lighthearted. "Something about cemeteries, maybe. Or endings. You sure you're all right?"

"I have to be."

When they got into the car, Laura put the keys in the ignition, then pulled a CD out of her purse. *Glenn Gould Plays Bach: Goldberg Variations*.

"A little gift."

"This is a first. Thanks."

"You could play it right now."

"Okay." Eugene opened the case and slipped the disc in. She started the engine as the music began.

"No talking, okay?" she said.

She drove south on Bayview into the Valley and up Pottery Road to the Danforth, heading back toward Woodbine. He could hear Gould's humming, could picture him hunched over as he played, his face close to his hands. The piece was calm and slow. Every note matched what Eugene saw through the window, the music transforming this ordinary scene of stores and businesses and people walking home in the grey dusk into something sublime.

She drove the last few blocks and stopped at the house where she was staying.

He turned the volume down. "It's beautiful."

"His music makes me want to keep living. I know that must sound unbelievable, but it's true." Laura let go of the steering wheel and put her hands on her lap. "I just wanted to say that I think, eventually, you'll find a way to move forward without your wife. You can hold on to a part of what you both shared together and still be ready for something new."

"That would be good. I could handle that." He glanced at her, sitting beside him in the darkened car. Only her mouth was visible in a band of street light. He knew it wouldn't be that easy. "I hope everything works out, Laura—your driving test too."

"I hadn't planned to actually take the test. But now I think I will. It'll be good for me. Anyway, thank you. I needed to do this with someone who doesn't know anything about me. You were patient. And kind." She held the door half open.

"Despite my lapse in good manners," Eugene said.

"All is forgiven." She smiled right at him, then got out.

He tried to think of something else to say but she was already walking to the porch. He looked at the house, watched as it swallowed her. Something was bothering him. A place missing from her tour. That video he'd borrowed from the library showed Glenn Gould out by the lake, all in black against the white of the snow. Tonight it would be freezing down there, the wind, relentless and cruel, but the view would be worth it.

He turned the volume back up and started driving, and as he listened, it felt as if Gould were playing the notes right then, right there. Eugene listened carefully and kept driving down the street past all the houses that seemed to huddle closer in the cold.

MAY DAY MAYDAY

———

this version:

It isn't a silent spring.

A single bird is calling, waking me. But it's dark. Three in the morning.

"Benny?" I turn to his side of the bed. Big inert lump of husband under the blankets.

Maybe the clock is wrong. No, a power out would leave it flashing 12:00. Maybe it's dark because it's raining. But if it's raining, wouldn't the bird be quiet? I lie there certain that sleep is now out of reach. Within reach is the post-apocalyptic novel on my bedside table. No, I'd much rather keep the light off. Let my mind eat away at my heart. Eat away at the comment that had accompanied the rejection of my single foray into creative writing, a woeful story of an urban family braving environmental collapse: "Ending not believable"—the phrase like a finger poking my back all day and now at night too. The other part of the comment, "in an otherwise hilarious farce," is merely confounding, given the story's sombre intent.

My cell starts vibrating on the bedside table. A text from our son Carson: *u wake? dum brd at wndw wont sht up!*

It's the wacky neighbourhood cardinal that goes bananas every May. Delirious, loony bird. Letting us know that even though it's spring, season of hope, the natural world is still messed up. All is normal.

or this version:

It is a silent spring, far north of the city on a corner of my cousin's acreage. We've fashioned a cabin of sorts from an old billboard advertising a golf course. We'll figure out more permanent shelter when we have to. Winter is many months and worries away. Meantime we forage for edible roots, ration our tinned foods, try our hand at propagating fruit trees on the property. Benny's teaching Carson how to chop the trunks of fallen trees into firewood and into makeshift furniture. Our life couldn't be more different than a month ago when the food shortages started, when people stopped smiling, stopped working, stopped leaving their homes or never returned to them. I had been reading the flood of online news updates when Carson came into the room one day with such solemnity that I turned from the screen to finally face him.

"Dad's eyes are red," he'd said, "and I'm scared."

Benny was likely choking up in front of the karaoke machine in the basement. That's where he'd been hiding. Singing sad songs. My stomach was in my throat, but breathing seemed frivolous anyway. I threw my arms around Carson.

Packing didn't take long. We grabbed the boxes of food and essentials I'd always kept ready. The body of the car sank. We could get nothing more in but ourselves. The roads were clogged and the day was ending by the time we reached open country. The evening sky bled pink and orange. In silence we stared through the windshield at the cartoon sunset, at this ironic spectacle of nature's beauty. We drove and drove and drove.

or this one:
It isn't a silent spring if people are out strolling. May is shy with warmth, the first real hint of summer on its way. It's still light out long after dinner. People slow to a stroll and linger along the Danforth. Like they're wearing the evening in place of the coats they shed earlier in the day. Only good things seem possible. Cars roll to a stop at red lights as if that is just fine, a chance to prolong a perfect day.

I walk with my jacket open, round stomach showing. I am introducing my baby to the world. *Check it out first from the safety of the womb, my child, a gradual introduction. Advance apologies for this world that will be your future.* What a wonder that a mistake was even possible at my advanced age. And, a girl. She will be my Rachel. Her birth the ultimate gesture of optimism in the face of bleakness. I have to believe she will get to grow up. Do something amazing one day. Carson, twelve, and aged beyond his years by bleak news of our degraded planet, agrees. Benny's just plain happy. A baby.

We are still in the house. We still have the car. The stores still have food. Benny still hopes to land a job. Carson still goes to school and blogs with other do-gooders about how to save us. Our neighbourhood is still a community. In this version decency prevails. Each day we ignore the grim decline of the natural world as best we can, focusing instead on our own lives and the fiction of our own importance.

This evening people pull chairs out of restaurants along the Danforth. Drinks in hand, they tilt their faces to catch the sun.

Closed eyes, a sweet sadness. I pass them all. I keep walking. I walk because stopping would break this pleasant trance, the moment's fragile hope.

no, this version:
It is a silent spring. I can sequester my family in the house but nothing in nature exists in isolation. We depend on the world outside. This is the news the wind carries. Barging through the open front door, the wind brings dead leaves, fragile corpses that scratch along the hallway toward the kitchen where I stand preparing the casserole. The sky has turned the colour of dyed oranges—impossible to know what might happen next: heavy rain or no rain for weeks. Gales that will pull the house apart or slam it with debris. Maybe only a summer breeze to coax us out into the heat.

The door is open and in creeps an albino squirrel and the older gentleman from up the street who wanders. They need refuge from the orange world outside. I close the door. Benny is in the basement and Rachel is kicking in my womb and Carson is upstairs on the computer. I slide the casserole into the oven and set the timer, countdown to the family meal.

The gentleman settles on the living room couch, hands on his knees, face blank, forgetting his seventy-five years. The white squirrel climbs the stairs to Carson's room. It has visited before, lured by his potted plants and leafy tree branches in water-filled pickle jars, foliage that brushes my arms when I clean. These inside branches, unlike the ones outside, stay green. Carson, online all day, likes to Photoshop Kim Jong Un: pasting that sour face onto the body of the world's second-tallest free-standing structure. They say that man is all bluster but it doesn't matter: if not him, then others wait in the wings, ready to terrorize. Carson sends funny Kim Jong Un images to friends and watches slapstick internet videos, waiting for their replies. At least he is home. At least he is safe.

Pleasant aroma from the oven. Kitchen clock hums the passage of time. The front hall glows with amber sunlight—attractive, though worrisome.

I call down the basement stairs to Benny. "The sky's an odd colour," I say.

He doesn't hear. He's starting another song on the karaoke. A song about telephones, opera houses and favourite melodies. Surrounded by posters of seventies singers, flipped hair and shiny lips, perennially young. He stands for hours on the concrete floor, microphone in hand. He sings that earth is really dying. Five years left to cry in.

The kitchen darkens. I freeze. Brace myself and peek through the curtains. A line worker on a ladder against a pole. Branches sway. A lemon yellow sky. I go to the front door to look. Out onto the porch. Faces peer from houses as the trees lose more unfurled leaves to the wind. I take a step, foot propelling forward, shoe slapping pavement. The other foot follows, and I'm moving down the road. The wind hisses. Some people are out and gardening or checking their mailbox as though everything was normal. Their denial stuns me, locks down my thoughts. And then I'm running. I run to the end of the block and turn. I run to the end of the block and turn. Again and again until I am back. In front of my home. My hand on the doorknob, and it opens on its own. Out comes the old gentleman. I'm surprised at our reversed positions at my door.

From the man's suit pocket the squirrel's pink eyes stare up into mine. What does this creature make of the changes? Leaves inside buildings, naked branches outside. What is it like to live in a tree through heat waves and savage storms?

"The sky has gone strange again," I say. "I don't know what to prepare for."

"Don't bother with all of that." The old man strokes the squirrel behind its ears. "Your son was asking about his dinner."

"He's growing so fast."

"It's how it goes. Growing, growing, then gone." He smiles and leaves.

Inside, the house is fragrant, vibrating with the crescendo of Benny's heartfelt song, energized by Carson's tapping on the computer keyboard, hopeful with ceilings I painted sky-blue.

One more minute on the timer.

I lean to check the casserole I made for my family on a day I feared something too big to even imagine.

I check the casserole, trying to pull my thoughts back into this kitchen where something good is possible.

I have checked the casserole and the casserole is ready.

Dinner is ready and now is the time to eat.

Acknowledgements

I am grateful beyond words to Stuart Ross for his generosity, enthusiasm, straight-shooting advice, eagle-eyed editing, and friendship. Never would I have guessed that the guy selling his books on a Yonge Street sidewalk, which I purchased as a teenager, would usher my own book into being decades later. Thanks to Denis De Klerck for allowing me into the esteemed and fully functional Mansfield family. I'm delighted to be published in my hometown of Toronto where many of these stories are set.

Thanks to all who read and commented on these stories over the eight years they took shape, especially Anne Marie Elliott, Jann Everard, and Diana Gibbs, and, in the early years, the KASH reading group. I also owe a lot to the writers I studied with.

A huge salute to the literary journals and magazines and their editors who accepted many of these stories and continue to give new writers their first published pages. Different versions of these stories appeared first in *This Magazine*, *Event*, *Grain*, *The Dalhousie Review*, *The New Quarterly*, *The Fiddlehead* and *Taddle Creek*.

I am very grateful for funding received from the Toronto Arts Council.

I am also grateful for growing up in a book-filled house, where the weekly family outing was a trip to the library. I thank my dad, Stan Heinonen, for his wide-ranging interests and encyclopedic knowledge, and my late mother, Audrey Heinonen, the prolific reader, for showing me without telling that fiction makes life richer.

Thanks to my sons, Henry and Matthew Lee, for being great kids and now, great young men, and artists in their own right.

Thanks most of all to Eric Chin-Kwong Lee, for his untiring support and for all the pep talks and laughs and wonderful times that sustained me through years of working to become a writer. His love and understanding of how much this book means to me means everything.

A landscape architect by training, Sara Heinonen lives in Toronto. She lived briefly in Hong
Kong back in the day. Her short
fiction has appeared in numer-
ous literary journals. She is
working on a novel, just like you
are, even though short stories
are really where it's at.

Other Books from Mansfield Press

Poetry

Leanne Averbach, *Fever*
Nelson Ball, *In This Thin Rain*
George Bowering, *Teeth: Poems 2006–2011*
Stephen Brockwell, *Complete Surprising Fragments of Improbable Books*
Stephen Brockwell & Stuart Ross, eds., *Rogue Stimulus: The Stephen Harper Holiday Anthology for a Prorogued Parliament*
Diana Fitzgerald Bryden, *Learning Russian*
Alice Burdick, *Flutter*
Alice Burdick, *Holler*
Jason Camlot, *What The World Said*
Margaret Christakos, *wipe.under.a.love*
Pino Coluccio, *First Comes Love*
Gary Michael Dault, *The Milk of Birds*
Pier Giorgio Di Cicco, *The Dark Time of Angels*
Pier Giorgio Di Cicco, *Dead Men of the Fifties*
Pier Giorgio Di Cicco, *The Honeymoon Wilderness*
Pier Giorgio Di Cicco, *Living in Paradise*
Pier Giorgio Di Cicco, *Early Works*
Pier Giorgio Di Cicco, *The Visible World*
Salvatore Difalco, *What Happens at Canals*
Christopher Doda, *Aesthetics Lesson*
Christopher Doda, *Among Ruins*
Glenn Downie, *Monkey Soap*
Rishma Dunlop, *The Body of My Garden*
Rishma Dunlop, *Lover Through Departure: New and Selected Poems*
Rishma Dunlop, *Metropolis*
Rishma Dunlop & Priscila Uppal, eds., *Red Silk: An Anthology of South Asian Women Poets*
Ollivier Dyens, *The Profane Earth*
Jaime Forsythe, *Sympathy Loophole*
Carole Glasser Langille, *Late in a Slow Time*
Suzanne Hancock, *Another Name for Bridge*
Jason Heroux, *Emergency Hallelujah*
Jason Heroux, *Memoirs of an Alias*
Jason Heroux, *Natural Capital*
John B. Lee, *In the Terrible Weather of Guns*
Jeanette Lynes, *The Aging Cheerleader's Alphabet*
David W. McFadden, *Be Calm, Honey*
David W. McFadden, *What's the Score?*
Leigh Nash, *Goodbye, Ukulele*
Lillian Necakov, *The Bone Broker*
Lillian Necakov, *Hooligans*
Peter Norman, *At the Gates of the Theme Park*

Peter Norman, *Water Damage*
Natasha Nuhanovic, *Stray Dog Embassy*
Catherine Owen & Joe Rosenblatt, with Karen Moe, *Dog*
Corrado Paina, *The Alphabet of the Traveler*
Corrado Paina, *The Dowry of Education*
Corrado Paina, *Hoarse Legend*
Corrado Paina, *Souls in Plain Clothes*
Stuart Ross et al., *Our Days in Vaudeville*
Matt Santateresa, *A Beggar's Loom*
Matt Santateresa, *Icarus Redux*
Ann Shin, *The Last Thing Standing*
Jim Smith, *Back Off, Assassin! New and Selected Poems*
Robert Earl Stewart, *Campfire Radio Rhapsody*
Robert Earl Stewart, *Something Burned on the Southern Border*
Carey Toane, *The Crystal Palace*
Priscila Uppal, *Summer Sport: Poems*
Priscila Uppal, *Winter Sport: Poems*
Steve Venright, *Floors of Enduring Beauty*
Brian Wickers, *Stations of the Lost*

Fiction

Marianne Apostolides, *The Lucky Child*
Sarah Dearing, *The Art of Sufficient Conclusions*
Denis De Klerck, ed., *Particle & Wave: A Mansfield Omnibus of Electro-Magnetic Fiction*
Paula Eisenstein, *Flip Turn*
Marko Sijan, *Mongrel*
Tom Walmsley, *Dog Eat Rat*

Non-Fiction

George Bowering, *How I Wrote Certain of My Books*
Denis De Klerck & Corrado Paina, eds., *College Street–Little Italy: Toronto's Renaissance Strip*
Pier Giorgio Di Cicco, *Municipal Mind: Manifestos for the Creative City*
Amy Lavender Harris, *Imagining Toronto*
David W. McFadden, *Mother Died Last Summer*

To order Mansfield Press titles online, please visit mansfieldpress.net